"Hey, Teach, wanna neck?"

Trace looked as if his mood matched his playful words, but Morgan was consumed by anxiety.

"I'm not sure," she answered honestly. "I don't know how to behave anymore. I might disappoint you."

"All right, let's investigate this, detective style," Trace replied gently. He lowered his lips to hers, no longer playing. After a moment, just when she felt overwhelmed by delicious sensations, he raised his head. "I don't know the rules of becoming involved with pillars of the community, either," he said, moving his hand across her sensitive nipples. "We'll just play it by ear. . . ."

Morgan couldn't help responding to his caress. Her senses had been reawakened, and she lon… for more of his taste, his scent, his …

"Anyway, i… first time,… always pr…

D1024618

Gayle Corey discovered romance books when she was still trying to cope with both part-time teaching and sleep deprivation, thanks to her two small children. With the birth of her third child, she threw in the supermom towel and decided to use nap time to write. *Top Marks* is Gayle's first romance novel, and we're delighted to welcome to Temptation a writer so obviously talented.

Like Morgan, the heroine of *Top Marks*, Gayle has taught nutrition at the college level, and now uses her own very practical experience to teach parenting courses. She lives in Okemos, Michigan, with her veterinarian husband, their children and a never-ending parade of animals.

Top Marks

GAYLE COREY

Harlequin Books

TORONTO • NEW YORK • LONDON
AMSTERDAM • PARIS • SYDNEY • HAMBURG
STOCKHOLM • ATHENS • TOKYO • MILAN

Published April 1988

ISBN 0-373-25300-1

Copyright © 1988 by Elaine Havptman. All rights reserved.
Philippine copyright 1988. Australian copyright 1988.
Except for use in any review, the reproduction or utilization of this work in whole or in part in any form by any electronic, mechanical or other means, now known or hereafter invented, including xerography, photocopying and recording, or in any information storage or retrieval system, is forbidden without the permission of the publisher, Harlequin Enterprises Limited, 225 Duncan Mill Road, Don Mills, Ontario, Canada M3B 3K9.

All the characters in this book have no existence outside the imagination of the author and have no relation whatsoever to anyone bearing the same name or names. They are not even distantly inspired by any individual known or unknown to the author, and all incidents are pure invention.

The Harlequin trademarks, consisting of the words, TEMPTATION, HARLEQUIN TEMPTATION, HARLEQUIN TEMPTATIONS, and the portrayal of a Harlequin, are trademarks of Harlequin Enterprises Limited; the portrayal of a Harlequin is registered in the United States Patent and Trademark Office and in the Canada Trade Marks Office.

Printed in U.S.A.

1

"DAMN IT, LADY. Did you hear me? I flunked the exam." The large, sandy-haired, rugged-looking man, with eyes almost too vividly blue to be real, leaned across her desk only inches away from her face.

"Yes, I did hear you," the slender, dark-haired, young woman in the smoke-colored wool suit replied dispassionately, coolly meeting the man's stormy glare. It was taking Dr. Morgan Harris a good deal of determined effort to keep from leaning back and averting her eyes. However, she was careful to appear detached and totally in charge. If she showed a moment's weakness he'd probably hound her forever for a few lousy points. She hated this particular scene, but she'd learned long ago that it was impossible to avoid when you taught large undergraduate classes.

Taking a deep breath through flared nostrils and straightening so he no longer leaned over her, the blue-eyed man made a visible, and not quite successful, effort to control his temper. "I picked up my test score today, and according to your printout, I did not pass the exam. Exactly how do you get by with flunking people in a class like this?"

"By being the instructor. That gives me the right to set the standards for passing, or not passing, any class I teach. However, don't take it personally. You're not alone. I flunked seventeen other people, too." Not nice, but it had been a long day, and frankly she was sick to death of being nice to whiny students trying to shift the responsibility for their poor grades onto her. Not that this one was exactly whining. In fact, this irate man, with his almost militarily styled short hair, and his unstudentlike sports jacket and slacks, didn't look much like a student.

The week after exams was the worst. Sometimes it seemed as if half the class felt obliged to come in and complain or argue about one thing or another. What did they expect her to do—give them some magic formula that would enable them to pass the class without cracking a book? Probably. Maybe when they all went home for Thanksgiving next week their parents would remind them that they were here for more than the football games.

"You flunked two dozen people?" he questioned tightly, his incredibly intense blue eyes watching her with a concentration that made her put a little extra effort into appearing unapproachable.

"Eighteen," she corrected. "That is an improvement over the first exam. Twenty-nine people failed to pass that one." Leaning back in her chair, she carefully bit back a smile at the look of chagrin that crossed his face. She was starting to enjoy this, which definitely meant it was time for her to go home and let her horde humble her. When you found your understanding-teacher mode slipping into sadistic student baiting, it was time for a dose of reality. Pulling her professional mantle back into place, she asked, "How did you do on that one?"

"I don't know. I haven't picked it up yet," the large man muttered, showing the decency to look at least a little sheepish and shift his uncomfortable blue eyes off her for a brief moment.

"Do you want me to look it up? I have the grade sheets here," she volunteered indifferently. Any chance he had had of gaining her sympathy had just died. Halfway through the fall semester, even the greenest freshmen had learned to keep at least a cursory eye on their grades as they drifted from party to party.

"Yes," he agreed, somewhat reluctantly. "My name's Trace Standon." Moving with surprising grace for a man his size, he sat down on the chair in front of her.

"I don't have this by name. You will need your student number," she replied with an arrogance that almost made her cringe when she heard herself.

Morgan froze momentarily in wary dismay. Apparently she had gone one step too far. This man had obviously had it with the depersonalization that the university, along with its professors, was such a master at. If his expression was anything to go by, she was going to reap the rewards for the whole hypocritical system, too.

The irritated man was no longer irritated. She wasn't exactly sure how to describe his expression. His irritation had shifted to something more rigidly controlled, considerably harder and far less understandable than mere anger. He seemed to have accepted a challenge she hadn't been aware of issuing. She frequently got that look from her son Matt. Only Matt was a novice and this man was an artist, she thought, as the sensitive hairs on the back of her neck rose. He leaned back in the chair and watched her methodically as if calculating her strengths and weaknesses for the upcoming battle. Swallowing hard, Morgan forced herself to appear reserved and composed as she looked up the number he rattled off at a clip that reminded her of a machine gun.

"You did not pass that one, either, I'm afraid, Mr. Standon." She folded her hands serenely and waited anxiously for his next move.

"How many students do you normally flunk out of this class?" he asked in a way that managed to strip her of any sense of power her academic position might have given her.

"Usually about fifteen to twenty end up with a failing final grade."

"Do you have any idea why I would have been told that this class was a cinch, and all I'd have to do is show up for tests to pass it?"

Morgan's large brown eyes became even larger. Someone had done a number on this guy. Her class was supposed to be a freshman class, but she typically had a large number of seniors who had put it off until the last possible semester because it was rumored to be so difficult. As the only "hard" science class many of the Home Economic and Family Child Development students needed to take, a few did find it totally incomprehensible but the majority did fine. "No, I was not aware that my class had that reputation. It's not a particularly difficult class if you stay on top of the material, but it is far from a guaranteed four credits," she answered honestly.

"Considering my grades so far, what would you suggest?" he asked, the harsh planes of his mature face becoming more pronounced as he clenched his back teeth.

What would she suggest? Jumping off a bridge. Arsenic, maybe. How about running in between the cars of a fast-moving train, Morgan thought grimly. "Drop the class," she told him flatly.

"I need the credits."

"Then sign up for it credit/noncredit so you'll only need a D to get credit, and then start working on learning the material."

"How do you suggest I go about catching up?" he asked almost sarcastically.

"Come to class, read the assignments, get hold of someone else's notes, study the old tests, and please feel free to set up an appointment with me to discuss any of the material you feel you don't understand." She rattled the list off as if she had gone through this a hundred times before, which probably was a fairly accurate estimate. *However, since you don't have an appointment now, and it is after five, please go away, scat, shoo, be gone, off with you,* she mentally urged him.

Instead of disappearing, he leaned back in his chair, the slight grin on his lips not softening his expression to any noticeable degree. "Good idea. We'll start tonight. I'll be over at your house at six-thirty."

"I think not," Morgan snapped in surprise. "I have office hours every Monday and Wednesday afternoon. You may set up an appointment then." She'd thought she'd heard them all. The first time she'd taught this class she'd been amazed at the number of college students who had their mothers call and make excuses for missed exams. One student even had her auto mechanic call. She'd had students cry, beg, threaten suicide, yell, offer her free football passes, and one enterprising soul had even offered to paint her house, all for a passing grade. She wasn't sure what this one was offering—a pass for a pass?

"Nothing's impossible, lady," his deep voice drawled smoothly.

"Studying at my house is," she informed him coldly. "Now if you will excuse me, I'm afraid I must be leaving."

Glancing out the corner of her eye as she packed her papers, she saw the relaxed man looking quite pleased with himself. He looked so satisfied with himself that she almost hoped he would show up. It was going to be such a zoo tonight, what was one more animal, more or less?

Morgan gave a private sigh of relief when she locked the office door. For a minute, she'd thought that he wasn't going to move. But he had. Now if he'd only step back far enough to quit breathing down her neck, she'd have no complaints. "Excuse me." She elbowed her way past him.

Much to her dismay, he fell into step beside her, shortening his smooth stride until it matched her brisk high-heeled clip. Morgan held her shoulders back and kept her head up. He was too big. At five foot seven, she wasn't used to men towering over her the way this one did. Maybe he wasn't all that huge exactly, she corrected when she shot a cold, professional, and hopefully intimidating look toward him. Six one at the most, and actually rather lean in a powerful, rangy kind of way. Something other than size gave him the self-confident presence that made her think that he was bigger than he actually was.

She took it back—even with the troops at home, she'd just as soon this one didn't join the ranks. Ten to one he'd want to be commander.

Stopping suddenly, Morgan turned to him with her most patronizing, haughty professor's voice. "Are you following me? If so, you may stop now."

A masculine grin slowly lightened his features. If his eyes had showed an equal trace of humor she would have been vastly reassured. But they didn't. Like arctic chips of blue ice, they started at the neckline of her suit and traveled down, stripping her slowly and completely.

"No, Doctor, I'm not following you. I'm escorting you to your car. It's late and getting dark. You never can tell what kind of thug might be lurking in the parking lot." His voice was a silken threat.

Morgan took an instinctive step away and looked around the hall quickly. Five-fifteen on a Friday night. The Nutritional Sciences building was absolutely dead. Bad word, she hastily corrected herself. Somewhere down in the bowels of this building, there would be a few dedicated graduate students buried in some lab weighing rat carcasses, but for all intents and purposes, she was alone with this suddenly very frightening man. Glancing up at him, she tried not to let her fear show. But it was hard.

Living in Lyons, Michigan, a medium-size, basically rural community, she'd never bothered to develop the protective reflexes necessary for life on an inner-city campus. But like all campuses, this one had its share of problems. And like all colleges, it had a newspaper that frequently warned women not to be alone in buildings or parking lots after dark.

Really studying her supposed student for the first time, not as a student who was trying to maneuver his way into a passing grade, but as the man who was scaring the stuffing out of her, she felt her throat constrict. He was probably pretty close to forty, and judging from the harsh planes of his face, it hadn't been a particularly easy forty years. He wasn't handsome—he was far too rugged for that description. He was wide shouldered and held himself with a loose grace that spoke of a tough, lean power. This very masculine man was also, she knew with horrible certainty, not in her class. Even with three hundred students she would have known if he had ever attended one of her lectures. This man didn't look as if he even belonged in the academic world she lived in.

Licking her suddenly dry lips, she forced herself to smile slightly. "Thank you, but I'm meeting a friend out by the fountain. He'll see me to my car safely. There's no reason for you to go out of your way."

With a sinking heart, she watched his grin widen with satisfaction. He knew she was lying. He also knew she was frightened. If she threw her books at him and ran as fast as she could, what were her chances of making it to her car? None, she answered herself, looking at the broad-shouldered male before her.

"It's no bother. I parked out in the teachers' lot myself. Illegally," he added, his grin widening a trifle.

Gulping for air, she nodded, then turned and resumed walking toward the stairs. *Think*, she prodded herself. There had to be some way out of this.

"Hey, Teach." He caught hold of her arm and turned her until she faced him. Draping both arms loosely over her shoulders, he bent his head so his eyes were only inches from hers. "You look scared to death."

For good reason, she thought grimly. Clasping her folders against her breast, she stared down at a button on his shirt, knowing she was a hair's breath away from outright panic.

He lowered his head until his forehead rested against hers. He dominated her senses completely. She felt scorched by the heat radiating from him. Every breath she took filled her with his essence, and his deep voice vibrated, almost incomprehensibly, around in her head. She felt imprisoned. His arms, resting lightly on her shoulders, held her as surely as if he were bruising her with his powerful hands.

"You're making me feel incredibly guilty," he complained, sighing softly. He kissed her on the tip of her nose. "What happened to that hard, cold, superior lady professor? The one that got such a charge out of running me down? Are you going to cry?" he asked with concern when he felt her shudder.

"No," she whispered weakly. "I'm going to throw up."

"Oh." He took a step back, still holding on to her shoulders. "Don't do that. I'm not going to hurt you. I never was. You just irritated me with your uppity-teacher routine." He started rubbing her shoulders. "I'm only going to walk you to your car. It really is getting dark."

Morgan believed him. He had lost that aura of danger that had surrounded him. Sometimes she honestly thought that she disliked men. They always had to be on top. Always had to turn things into a power struggle. Relief swept over her, but it was already too late. Frantically she shoved her folders into his chest, turned and ran, not toward the door, but toward the women's bathroom.

Washing the vile taste from her mouth, Morgan looked at herself in the mirror. It could be worse—she could have her mother's fair skin and now be all blotchy and red. Instead, her darker complexion that always looked tanned no matter how long the Michigan winters, just looked a little greenish yellow. She despised herself for throwing up. As a kid she had done it at the drop of a hat, causing her brothers endless amusement, Get Morgan upset and watch her puke. At thirty-two, though, she really ought to have a bit better control.

Pinning up a few shoulder-length strands of her dark chestnut hair that had slipped out of her businesslike bun, she gathered what she could of her pride and tentatively pushed open the door. With any luck at all, he would have been so grossed out that he'd have left her folders by the door and taken off. He could even keep the folders if he wanted, as long as he was gone. There was nothing that important about the grade sheets for some 350 students. She'd give them all As. That would cause her less grief than talking to one Trace Standon again.

Peeking through the half-opened door into the hallway, she couldn't see anyone. She'd taken only a couple of steps out of the rest room when her vertebrae fused into a rigid line as a deep voice, hinting amusement, came from behind her. "You forgot your things."

Turning stiffly to where he leaned casually against the wall, Morgan kept her eyes firmly fixed on his right shoulder and held her hands out for the folders. "Thank you. I can take them now."

"That's okay. I'll carry them for you." He pushed off the wall and took her by the arm as he started walking toward the stairs.

"You can relax now. I'm through picking on you." When she didn't respond, he tried again. "Hey, look, I'm an honest guy. I could have changed my grades while you were in there losing your lunch. But here they are, safe and sound."

"I would have remembered them," Morgan answered, a little irritated by the laughter she heard in his voice. She wasn't afraid of him anymore. Embarrassed silly, but not afraid. Exposed to twisted male humor all her life, she found it easy to believe that this was another weird joke.

"I bet. I'll probably be the only one in the class whose computer card gets lost on the next exam."

"Are you really in my class?" Morgan let her embarrassment fade. She'd played the fool before and she undoubtedly would again. It seemed a bit childish to be angry with him.

"Unfortunately, yes."

Biting back a smile, she asked, "Are you trying to butter me up with all this praise of my teaching abilities?"

"I hadn't thought about it. Do you suppose it's worth a try?" He smiled at her as he opened the outside door.

"Probably would beat making me throw up," she responded dryly.

Laughing, he took her arm again and headed for the parking lot. "Ah, Professor Harris, you're making me feel worse by being such a good sport about my rotten temper. Don't you think you should yell or at least pout?"

"You want me to throw a temper tantrum?" she asked easily, pulling her coat tighter around her when the cold hit her.

"No," he admitted, "but if you could be a little bit condescending again I could at least tell myself you deserved me."

"Sorry, I'll try to do better next time. Here's my car." Unlocking the door, she took her folders from him and slid onto the seat. "Thank you for walking me to my car. I think." She smiled ruefully up at him.

"Anytime, Professor. Anytime at all." Reaching down, he caught her seat belt, and pulling it out, he fastened it, managing to brush his hand across her hips. Smiling thoughtfully at her, he closed the car door and walked away without a backward glance.

BY THE TIME the doorbell rang a second time, Morgan felt she had to respond to it—in the middle of a diaper change or not. Making a mad run down the hall, she threw open the door, turned and ran back up the hall, yelling, "Just set them on the kitchen table! I'll get the money in a minute!"

A moment later she walked down the hall, drying her hands on the old and not particularly clean jeans she wore. "Twenty-four fifty, right?" she called toward the kitchen as she dug her checkbook out of her purse in the entry closet.

"Well, actually I wanted an A. Figured that would run me something more like seventy-two fifty." The familiar deep voice, which definitely did not belong to the pizza delivery kid, answered.

"What are you doing here?" She looked at her unwelcome visitor in unhappy surprise.

"You're lucky it was me. Do you always leave your front door unlocked and then open it to anyone who happens to ring the bell? Stupid thing to do, lady."

Taken aback by his attack on her, she stared at him a moment. "I was expecting someone else. What are you doing here, and how did you find out where I live?"

"It doesn't matter who you were expecting, it's who walks in the door that you have to worry about. A door isn't a lot of protection, but you might as well use it."

"Okay, I'm sorry. I promise to always look before I open the door. So why are you here?" she repeated. His lecture about her door-answering habits was either a ploy to throw her off the subject, or he took unlocked doors seriously. By the intensity of those blue blue eyes that looked down at her, she sincerely hoped he didn't notice that the dead bolt on the door was a fraud. C.J. had tried, but somehow the bolt didn't quite line up with the hole in the door frame, no matter what her brother had tried.

What was Trace Standon doing here, anyway? The last thing she needed was more company. Especially this kind of male company when she looked the way she did, she thought with frustration as she pushed her uncombed shoulder-length hair back from her face and wiped her still-damp hands on her pants again.

"I came to get started on our study sessions. Judging from my past performance, I don't have any time to lose. Hey, don't look so happy to see me. At least I came bearing gifts." He gestured toward a large pizza box on the table.

"What kind is it?" Morgan asked with the slightest hint of a smile.

"It's got everything but anchovies. Don't you like pizza?" he asked as a strange look flitted across her face.

"Love the stuff. But as I said before, it's impossible to study here."

"Anything is possible," he countered.

"Not studying here—at least not tonight." He was going to stay. She could see it in the determined set of his jaw. If any other student had shown up like this, she'd have had him out on his ear so fast that his head would have spun, but this attractive, mature male was a different matter. It might be fun to have some company tonight, at least until he found an excuse to run. Besides, it would serve him right for his lousy treatment of her.

"We'll see," he answered arrogantly. "I brought some wine to go with the pizza. Where are your glasses?" He walked to the cupboards and started going through them.

Watching him rifle her shelves, Morgan smiled. He had a very impressive set of shoulders. In fact, it was a very impressive-looking man standing in her kitchen. He looked good there. Too bad he wouldn't be staying long.

When the doorbell rang a second later, Morgan turned to answer it, only to have Trace move her out of the way. "I'll get it."

"What are you glaring at? I'm sure it's only the pizza boy," she told the man, who had turned from a good-looking kitchen decoration into a rather formidable protector at the sound of the doorbell.

"That's who you thought I was, too, remember?" he reminded her.

"Yes, and I was right. You did bring a pizza," she tossed back at him.

"Professor, did you order four large pizzas?" Trace called to her from the door.

"Yes. The check is already made out. It's on the shelf by my purse in the closet," she called back.

Entering the kitchen with the pizzas, he set them on the table. "Is this going to be self-explanatory, or should I ask the obvious?"

"Oh, it will make itself very clear in a few seconds." She laughed outright at his wary expression.

Walking to the basement door, she opened it and yelled, "Kids, the pizzas are here!"

"Kids?" a soft voice behind her echoed.

"Kids!" she yelled again, this time down the hall. "Dinner's ready! Come and get it!"

Any comment he might have made was lost in the sound of stomping feet, rebel yells and demands to stop shoving. Morgan watched the man's stunned expression with satisfaction as the room filled with kids ranging in age from two to fourteen. If seduction had been what he had had in mind when he showed up tonight, then he had just had his comeuppance.

She only had a moment to savor her revenge before she was wrapped up in answering demands of the children.

"Oh, wow. Double cheese. Mom, can we start?"

"Yes, go ahead."

"Yuck, look at this one. It's got all sorts of crud on it."

"I like that kind," a young voice defended Trace's offering.

"No, no, don't eat it. Don't you know why they put all that stuff on top?" At the others' look of ignorance the food connoisseur went on. "When they make the dough they have a big machine that squashes the little balls of dough into pizzas. Sometimes, just before the weight falls, a rat runs up and tries to eat the dough. Then splat, the dough and rat get squashed together. Those are the ones they put a lot of junk on in order to cover up the rat."

"Really?"

"Yes, it's a fact," her daughter assured him. "Look, see those brown things—" she pointed with obvious distaste to the mushroom pieces "—those are rat bits that have floated to the top."

"Oh, that is totally gross," the one-time mushroom lover groaned sickly.

As the kids went on to fight about who got what piece of pizza, Morgan joined the group. Setting down a plate with a pizza slice that had been cut up into small pieces, she looked up to see Trace watching her with a slightly dazed expression. Smiling at him, she reached around behind him and picked up the baby, setting her in the chair by the cut-up pizza. Sneaking another glance at him, she grinned wickedly.

The older kids had helped themselves to the cheese pizza and then they disappeared in various directions, leaving Morgan, the baby, a little girl about four, and Trace, who still stood where he had been when the kids had first descended.

"Do sit down, Mr. Standon. Please help yourself. We're not very formal around here," Morgan invited him around a bite of the pizza with everything.

Following her instructions silently, he picked up a piece of the pizza he'd brought and eyed it distrustfully.

"Go ahead. I took a bite and didn't taste anything like squashed rat," she encouraged him impishly. After he'd taken a big bite, she continued, "Of course, I didn't take my bite out of the middle—I only nibbled along the crust where I could see."

Looking at her grimly out of the corner of his eye he said dryly, "Professor, you are a fraud. And you can save those innocent looks, too. I'm on to you."

"Watch out for your arm," she warned Trace. "Kelly, honey, could you get a towel for Ann. She spilled her milk. Thank you. Here you go, Ann. You can take care of it," she told the two-year-old.

"How many kids do you have?" he asked curiously.

"Three," she answered distractedly as she moved from the path of the milk that was being energetically spread around the table.

"There are a lot more than three kids in this house," he commented, as he took another bite of pizza.

"How many would you guess?"

"Twelve?" He shrugged.

"Hope you do better than that on my other test questions. There are only eight." She grabbed another bite of her own pizza when it looked like the baby was occupied pulling the topping off her pizza pieces.

"Okay, I give up. Which ones are yours and why are all the others here?" He handed the older little girl another piece of pizza.

"Of the older six that were in here, the squashed rat is mine, my daughter verified the story, and Steven, my other son, was taking advantage of their lapse of attention to fill his plate. The other three are friends who are spending the night, and these two Munchkins are my nieces, who are also spending the night."

"I feel kind of left out," Trace complained. "Everyone is spending the night except me."

"You could sleep over with me," Kelly offered as she climbed onto his lap. "Daddy forgot my teddy bear."

"Thank you, honey, we'll see." The earnest expression on the young child's face seemed to make Trace a little uncomfortable.

"Of course, you would have to fit into the portable crib," Morgan teased.

"I'm a big girl. The baby bed is Ann's. I sleep in a big bed cause I only wet it sometimes," Kelly told her indignantly.

Looking with sudden distrust at the child on his lap, he seemed to come to some decision as a grimace of a smile crossed his face and he patted the child's leg. "The next obvious question is, where is your children's daddy?"

"Don't you think you should have asked that first, before you invited yourself to dinner?"

"You don't wear a ring." He shrugged.

"True, but maybe I just forgot to put it on today."

Grinning at her, he elaborated, "You also don't have a ring line around your finger, and if you had been married, it would have been your husband waiting for you out by the fountain. Enough?" He raised his eyebrows in question.

"Quite. Thank you," she let the professor in her answer, hoping to irritate him a little. His widening grin seemed to indicate that it hadn't worked.

"So where is Daddy?" he asked with a bit more force in his voice.

"With his wife, I presume," she answered coolly.

"What happened?"

Leaning back in her chair, Morgan looked at him, letting her expression tell him exactly what she thought of his snoopiness.

"Too pushy?" he asked a bit uncertainly.

"Oh, no, not at all," she assured him sarcastically. "Wait until things calm down here a bit and I'll dig out my diary for you to read."

Grinning sheepishly, he was saved from the necessity of responding by an influx of kids looking for seconds.

"Mom!" a voice yelled up from the basement. "That video you wanted to see is on!"

"Thanks!" she yelled back as she walked over into the attached family room and turned on the television.

Trace twisted his head to see what she was watching. Seeing what he was doing, Morgan's daughter helped him out.

"It's that lead singer of the Velvet Touch." She named a trendy rock group with an extremely feminine-looking male lead. "Mom loves him."

A couple of minutes later, Morgan returned to the table and sat down. Pulling the baby onto her lap, she tried to clean the pizza sauce off the messy face.

"You like that singer?" Trace asked with disbelief.

"Yes, he's kind of cute."

"You've got strange taste, lady." He shook his head at her.

"Yeah, Mom. He's real fag. Nobody likes him," her daughter informed her, her voice laden with all the disgust a ten-year-old can drag up for a mother, as she walked out of the room.

Trace turned toward Morgan with a surprised look of question. "Does she know what she's saying?"

"I hope not. If she does, I'm in a lot of trouble." Morgan sighed. "You see, not only is he fag, but so are my jeans, her brothers, the color of her room, taking showers at school and last winter's coat, which she promised me just twelve months ago that she would wear for years and years. Apparently that charming term is this weeks version of 'grody to the max.'"

"Mom, is there any dessert?" A delicate, dark-haired twelve-year-old boy popped his head around the basement door.

"Yes, make-your-own sundaes. Why don't you go get everyone and I'll set up?"

"Great." Steven leaped into the kitchen letting loose an ear-piercing rebel yell, followed by an equally loud cry of, "Dessert's on!"

"Good grief, Steven, I could have done that myself," Morgan complained to her son.

"Really? When did you learn to give a rebel yell?" he asked innocently, just managing to dodge the wet dishcloth his mother tossed at him.

The rest of the evening was equally chaotic. Worse actually, Morgan admitted, since the kids had chosen to eat dessert in the kitchen with them. Between friends and food, the kids pretty much ignored Trace except, Morgan noticed with trepidation, Matt, who sounded Trace out on whether he was afraid of rats or snakes or anything like that. The downright predatory look on Matt's face made it quite clear that she was going to end up paying for her sins. Maybe not with Trace—she couldn't see him allowing himself to be exposed to her family after tonight—but Lord help any man who tried to date her.

About ten o'clock Morgan and Trace found themselves deserted and sitting on the couch. The babies were in bed, and the older children were watching the last half of a horror film they had picked up that day.

"Is your house always like this?" the relaxed man asked easily.

"This is a bit worse than usual. Everybody is showing off a little for their friends, but it is a madhouse a lot of the time." Morgan sat, slouched down on the couch with her stocking feet resting on a coffee table, sipping the wine she was finally getting around to.

"Dinner here is quite an experience." His lips twisted ruefully.

"I'm kind of surprised that you didn't turn and run when you first saw the kids. You probably deserve some sort of award for staying this long. I like them, but they got to me when they were babies and my maternal hormones made it impossible for me to make a rational decision." She smiled fondly.

"Oh, I don't need an award. I was thinking of some other kind of recognition."

Morgan lifted her head at the seductive tone of his voice. Looking at him, she saw that his eyes had the same expression as his voice. Quieting a touch of nervousness, she grabbed a folder from the table beside her. "Oh, yes, I'd forgotten that you wanted to study. Okay, try this. What is the relationship between pancreatic function and vitamin A?"

"Try another one," Trace suggested after a very brief hesitation.

"Tell me about vitamin E toxicity." When no answer was forthcoming, she looked at the man who had laid his head back and was staring up at the ceiling. She closed the folder. "You didn't even read it, did you?"

"Not yet, but I was giving serious consideration to the idea of buying the book."

Releasing an unladylike snort, she picked up a book from the table and tossed it to him. "I think you had better borrow one of mine. I doubt the bookstore even has any more this late in the semester."

Catching her book easily, he thumbed through it. "If I take your book, what are you going to use? I don't want to read it if you're going to have to take all your questions from your lectures."

"Lord give me strength." Morgan took another sip of wine and rolled her eyes heavenward. "I don't want to pry, but how are you planning on passing my class? Just curious, you understand—nothing personal."

"Oh, I'll come up with something." He glanced at her, his eyes brimming with laughter. "Anyway, private tutoring in nutrition was not exactly the reward I was looking for."

"Unless you want something like another glass of wine, it's the best reward I can come up with." Morgan smiled a little nervously.

"I'm glad to see that I'm not the only one around here who can't come up with the right answer," he teased, reaching over and pulling her closer until she sat on his lap.

Seeing her fearful, nervous expression, the tawny-haired man gave a twisted smile. "Shh, quiet now, Professor. Everything is all right, I'm not going to force anything on you. I'm just going to kiss you. No biggie—just a first-date kiss." He lowered his lips to hers and started gently nibbling on her lower lip.

A first-date kiss. She'd never had a first-date kiss. She'd always been the third- or fourth-date kiss type, and she rarely went out with anyone that many times. But this was a nice kind of kiss. Relaxing in the light circle of his arms, she let herself enjoy the kiss. She probably ought to make him stop, and for some unknown reason she was sure she would not have any difficulty getting him to stop, but it was such a nice kiss. Or at least it would have been a nice kiss if he'd stopped messing around and had gotten down to business, she thought as he caught her lower lip between his teeth and nibbled on her delicately.

The teasing touch of him made her hungry for a real kiss. Sliding her arms up to the back of his neck, she played with the very short dense hair at his nape, finally weaving her fingers together and pulling him closer to her. Knowing what she wanted, he flicked his tongue over her lips once again in a teasing gesture before he met her in a solid, satisfying kiss. Using his tongue as a gentle probe, he silently asked permission to explore her further. She parted her lips, granting his request. As he tasted the sensitive contours of her mouth, Morgan felt her body tighten as a wave of pure lust rocked her.

She hadn't been with a man for years. She hadn't even wanted a man. But she recognized that in all honesty she wanted this man—wanted him badly. That realization helped her to pull back from the seductive web he was weaving around her. Her living room, in a house filled with children, was not the place to decide whether to change some long-standing life patterns.

Sighing into the warm sensuality of his mouth, she lowered her arms from around his neck back to his shoulders and moved her head slightly to let him know she wanted him to stop. Acquiescing to her unspoken request, he slowly lightened the kiss until he was again nibbling on her lips.

"Dear Teach, what am I lacking in my diet that is making my ears ring?" he asked, his voice heavy with passion.

"Vitamin E, maybe. Whatever it is, it's making my eyes want to close." Gently she ran her hand over the muscles on his back, calming herself, while at the same time satisfying an unexpected need to touch him. Her hand had reached about midway down his back when everything went sour.

He was wearing a gun. Through the fabric of his sport coat, her fingertips gently made out the shape of a gun harness strapped around his shoulder. She'd never felt one before, but she knew exactly what it was. Shifting her body slightly, she was sure she felt the hard metal of the gun pressed against her ribs. What had she done? Of the many possibilities that flashed through her mind as to why a man would wear a gun to bring his teacher a pizza, none of them boded well.

"Please let me go." She stirred in his arms. "The kids could walk in."

"Yeah, I guess you're right. I'm not used to being around kids. They must cramp your style." Reluctantly he lifted her off his lap and set her beside him, his arm again draped casually across her shoulders.

Style? She didn't have any style. She'd never done anything like this before and she never would again, if she could get this man and his gun out the door. "I hate to run you off, but I have to get the other kids to bed, and I'm tired myself."

"All right, Professor, I'll let you get on with your duties. But I don't think that this is something we should drop right here. I want to see you again."

"Sure. Now is just not the time." *We can get together the next time hell freezes over. Please leave; please just leave*, she begged silently.

Draping an arm around her shoulders, he walked her to where he had hung his coat in the closet. He was putting on his overcoat when Matt popped out of the basement.

"Mom, is there any popcorn left?" he asked.

"No, go back downstairs with your friends. Right now, Matt," she snapped.

"Mom?"

"Now, Matthew," she ordered with as much authority as she could muster.

"Geez," he griped as he disappeared down the stairs.

"Hey, lady, we didn't do anything all that scandalous." Trace took her chin in his hand and gently forced her to look at him. "Are you all right?"

"Yes, fine. I'm just tired. Please go." She bit the inside of her lip to stop it from trembling.

"Professor?" he questioned softly.

"Just go, please," she whispered. He probably thought she was nuts, but if his thinking she had bats in her belfry would make him leave, that would be fine with her.

"If you're sure." He kissed her on the cheek. "Check that the door is locked after I leave."

"I will," she replied.

Making herself close the door slowly instead of slamming it the way she wanted to, she locked it and leaned her back against it.

"Mom, what's the matter with you, anyway?" Matt had come back upstairs.

"Nothing, hon. I'm sorry I yelled at you. Who's still awake down there?" She tried to make her voice sound normal.

"Oh, the little kids are all asleep," he said dismissively of his brother and sister who were all of one and three years younger than he. "It's just Kevin and me."

"Good. I think I'm going to bed, too. Good night, hon." Turning to walk down the hall, she stopped and looked at her son. "If you should hear anyone knocking or anything like that tonight, please come get me right away."

"Mom, you're acting really weird. What's wrong?"

"Nothing. I guess your movie made me a bit edgy, and all I did was listen to you talk about it."

"Yeah, it was great. You should have seen it. I bet you would have barfed."

"Wonderful. Good night, Matt."

2

MORGAN GLANCED at her watch again. She had about fifteen minutes to get herself together for the basic nutrition lecture. Chances were she would not be able to do it. After all, she had tried all weekend to make some sense out of Friday night and hadn't yet succeeded.

It did not stand to reason that the man—who had seemed legitimately concerned because a two-year-old girl had yelled no to everything he had tried to put on her sundae, and had then cried because he gave her plain ice cream—had come to her house with something evil in mind. He was definitely flunking her class, but he didn't seem particularly concerned about it. Irritated perhaps, but nothing in his behavior indicated he thought it was a life-or-death matter. He had been fun, and darn it, she had liked him.

It was not as if he was the only man in the world to be attracted to her. She knew she was reasonably attractive. With her high cheekbones, almost coppery toned skin, dark chestnut shoulder-length straight hair, and large very dark brown eyes, she was frequently taken for a member of some exotic race. When the department was filling out their affirmative action report they had tried to get her to admit to being American Indian or Eurasian. She'd had to show them a picture of her blond-haired, blue-eyed mother and brothers before they had reluctantly admitted that she couldn't even be classed as an "other."

Tall, slender, and pretty easygoing about things, she'd had men in her life. But without exception they fell into the class of casual friends. They would start out being interested in her as a woman, find out she was in no hurry to jump into bed, meet her children and immediately decide that she would make a fine platonic friend. Soon her life and theirs would become too busy for even friendship, and they became friendly acquaintances.

She couldn't blame them. Once she had been playing around with a statistics program on her computer and had calculated how many different interactions existed in a family of five—it had come to 683. Given that, she'd have thought twice before she got involved with her family, too.

Her kids weren't the easiest to be around, either. Basically they were good kids, and if they lived to adulthood, she had little doubt that they would be stable, fine people. Occasionally she had to question their chances of ever reaching adult status.

Matt was probably the hardest. The tall, black-haired boy, who at this stage in his life was all gangly arms and legs, was so bright that he sometimes scared her. However, at thirteen he showed a formidable intelligence that wasn't always so well directed. The divorce had been hard on him, too. He'd been seven, old enough to really feel the loss of family, but not old enough to understand that he wasn't to blame. He had spent the next year seemingly trying to prove to everyone that, yes indeed, he was a rotten-enough kid to drive a father away. To some extent he'd succeeded, and unfortunately some of that aggressive, combative behavior had stuck. The custody battle a couple of years ago had brought it all out again.

That one had been hard on everyone. The kids had stood beside her, staunch supporters during the mess, but afterward all their fears and insecurities had come out full force. Life had been rough around her house for a while.

Baby-faced Amanda, who was just beginning to show some hint of the beauty she would probably develop into, was still being manipulated by that woman Simon had married. Thanks to Amanda's stepmother's vindictiveness, Morgan and her ten-year-old daughter had a highly charged love-hate relationship. At least the boys were not involved with those battles. How about that, she thought ruefully, there was some advantage to having active, rambunctious, aggressive boys. Their stepmother could not stand to be around them for five minutes. Maybe Morgan should teach Amanda to break windows and perch on the backs of couches.

With his wavy ginger hair and his angelic face, Steven was the easiest of the three, but sometimes he made her the most nervous. At twelve, he was funny, happy, and mercenary as all get-out. He undoubtedly had more money than she, and she hated to think of the ways he'd earned it. Nothing illegal generally, but was it normal for a kid to charge his sister for not beating her up? Morgan stifled his more dubious enterprises regularly, but he seemed to have unlimited creativity and more than enough energy and ambition to begin new money-making ventures as soon as the old ones folded.

There were lots of reasons why she was a good buddy to the men she knew. Some of the reasons had nothing to do with kids, either, she admitted. In fact, if she had to be totally honest, she knew she was not above hiding behind her kids. She'd been married so young and thrown into motherhood so quickly that she really didn't know how to handle men as anything but friends or co-workers. Any other role made her a bit nervous. She was never quite sure what to do around men, and tended to try to turn everything into some kind of joke. She wasn't very sophisticated for a thirty-two-year-old woman.

Simon had accused her of being cold and uninterested sexually. She'd always supposed she was that way because he was such an inconsiderate lover and husband, but maybe he had been right. She'd lived without physical involvement for a number of years, and until last Friday, she hadn't really missed that.

Not long ago, she had gone out with a man a few times and he had seemed interested in her family. Maybe a little too interested, Morgan thought grimly. No, all in all, she and hers were better off with just each other, rocky as it was at times. When all the kids were off on their own, she promised herself, she would take a cruise to the South Seas and fall in love.

Glancing at the clock again, she winced slightly. She'd spent the past fifteen minutes establishing that her kids were rotten and she was a frigid coward, and now, without any plan in mind, she had to walk into a lecture hall where a man with a gun might or might not be waiting.

Feeling small and vulnerable, Morgan looked around the large lecture hall. There were almost four hundred seats, but from where she stood in the center of the half circle, she could see that Trace wasn't there. In fact, a whole lot of people weren't there. Nothing like giving an exam to reduce attendance. However, she knew that the closer she got to the next exam, the more students would find it convenient to attend lectures.

Morgan was about halfway through the lecture when a door at the top of the room opened and Trace slipped into a chair at the back. Half expecting him to pull out a gun and shoot her, she stopped talking and stood mute, gaping at him. When he grinned and subtly waved his hand, she woke up and realized her class was watching her expectantly.

Only grim determination got her through the next half hour. When the buzzer finally went off, Morgan managed to be the first one out the door. In full retreat, she made it up the stairs back to her office. Finally safe, she sat at her desk and cradled her head in her hands.

Maybe she should call the police. They seemed to be the logical ones to handle this. The only trick was going to be what she would tell them. One of my students threatened me outside my office last week.... No, officer, he didn't really say anything.... No, he didn't touch me. He did give me a dirty look, though. Anyway, then after dinner at my home... Of course I didn't invite him—he just showed up, so I fed him. When we were rolling around together on the couch, I discovered he was wearing a gun.... No, he didn't threaten me with it.... What did he do? Well, I asked him to leave and he promptly left.... But, officer, there really *is* a problem. The man is now attending the class that he is registered for. The scene lacked a certain credibility.

When the doorknob rattled, Morgan looked up, horrified. She had forgotten to lock the door. It was only three days ago she'd been bawled out for that very same thing. Stupid, stupid, stupid.

"Hi, Professor," Trace's deep voice greeted her from the doorway. "You can make it out of a crowded room and up a flight of stairs faster than anyone I know. Running away from something?"

"Trace." She looked up at him. The sight of this large, rugged, possibly armed man standing in front of her made her long for an opportunity to call the police and make a fool of herself.

"I'm impressed—got the name right off," he teased her, with a curious glance at her. Closing the office door behind him, he sat in the chair in front of her and stretched his legs out comfortably.

Running her tongue along her suddenly dry lips, she managed to choke out, "Is there something I can do for you?"

"You're sounding like a teacher again, Morgan."

He was watching her closely, Morgan thought. Much too closely. "Oh, um, sorry," she apologized weakly, looking down at her desk to avoid those too-observant eyes that never left her face.

"Sorry for what? Kissing me?"

"I'm sorry for sounding like a teacher," she mumbled, mortified that she now sounded more like a child than a teacher.

"Good. If you're not sorry about kissing me, then let's discuss when we can get together again," he said.

"Get together?" Her voice came out a squeaky whisper.

"Morgan, what is the matter with you? You were fine Friday. Why are you acting like you're afraid of me now? I'm the same person who dried dishes for you last week."

Morgan's eyes flew up to his face. It was amazing. The man could go from something that would scare Godzilla back into the water into a Mr. Rogers in a twinkling. Without stopping to think, she blurted out, "Why did you bring a gun to my house?" Stunned by the words that had actually left her mouth, she stared at him wide-eyed.

Shaking his head slightly, he flashed her a telling look and, reaching into his pants pocket, pulled out his wallet. "That's why you acted so strange after I kissed you. I thought maybe you were having second thoughts. I suppose I should be lucky you didn't throw up again. Or did you?" His eyes pinned her.

Shaking her head, she picked up the wallet he'd opened and tossed on her desk. "You're a cop?" she asked in disbelief.

"A detective with the police. Close enough to cop, I guess." He leaned back in his chair and with a satisfied grin watched her.

Swallowing hard, she looked back down at the wallet. "You could have told me," she accused him quietly.

"I never knew it was an issue. Are you crying? Morgan, what did you think I was? Some insane student out to get you for flunking me on some lousy test?" He got up and moved around to her side of the desk. Once there he caught her by her shoulders and lifted her to her feet. He answered his own question as he looked into her eyes. "Yes, that's exactly what you thought I was. I don't know whether I want to wring your neck or kiss you to make you better."

"If I get a vote, I'll take the kiss," she whispered in a weak attempt to turn this into a joke and maybe save a little face. A cop. No, a detective. That possibility hadn't even crossed her mind.

"You're probably right. After all, you're the professor." He slid his arms around her so one hand was on her shoulder blades and the other was on the small of her back. With a gentle, sure pressure he pulled her closer to him.

Her large brown eyes full of unshed tears, she watched his lips come closer until they were just a blur. A sigh escaped her when he started to sprinkle seductive little butterfly kisses on the corner of her mouth, working up to her closed eyes and back down to her lips. Back at his starting point, he claimed her lips with a sureness that did a whole lot more than make her feel better.

His arms tightened, molding her against the hard planes of his body. Lowering his hand to the fullness of her buttocks, he cradled her firmly and intimately against his leg, which he had worked between hers.

His clean scent filled her, and her body instinctively softened to accommodate his. Morgan relaxed and accepted his passionate caresses. He was so strong and so real. She always had to be the strong one. That quality came with being a single mother. Be strong or the whole family flounders. It was almost a relief to relinquish her strength to this male. For a moment out of time, she clung to his hard shoulders, letting him make all the decisions.

All too soon he ended the kiss. Lifting his lips from hers, he tucked her head under his chin and held her tightly, rocking them both gently from side to side.

"You know, Prof, this is not a whole lot more private than your house," he murmured.

"Guess not," she agreed, without particularly caring about anything but the solid feel of him.

"When you said you would see me again, did you mean it, or were you just getting some mad-dog killer away from your kids?" Rubbing her back, he lowered his large hand to explore the contours of her derriere.

"Mostly I was getting rid of you." Morgan sighed and, turning her head slightly, kissed his chest through his shirt.

"Since it obviously didn't work, maybe you should plan on meeting me?" Trace tightened his grip on her and lifted her up slightly so she could feel the unmistakable sign of his arousal against her soft belly.

Closing her eyes, Morgan let the warm waves of desire cover her like a comforting blanket. He felt so good. She hadn't felt like a sensual person in such a long time. Sighing loudly, she forced herself back into the real world where she had so many others to think about that her wants naturally took second or even third place. "Trace, this is probably going to come as a real surprise to you, but I never do this kind of thing." She nuzzled a little closer to him, savoring his touch for a moment longer. "With my kids and all, it's better that I don't get involved with men. I'm going to wait until they all move away from home."

His voice was laced with laughter when he answered, "Now that makes good sense to me. What's ten years or so to a cold-blooded lady like yourself?"

"Ten years?" Morgan could almost see the wave of black depression about to settle on her.

"Since you're not going to go in for this kind of thing, I guess we'll have to get together and just study." He rotated her slight hips against him in a little circle.

"Guess so. You forgot to take the book home with you the other night, anyway." She felt like crying. Why did her life have to be so darned complicated? She had the ominous feeling that when Trace moved into that vast no-man's territory of casual friend, she was going to miss him a lot more than she had the others.

"Sounds good. I'll come by tomorrow night and pick it up. All right with you?" He kissed her neck.

"Yes, as long as you remember we have a platonic relationship," she murmured halfheartedly, tipping her head back to allow him greater access to the sensitive area on her neck.

"Morgan, you are insane, but I'll still stop by." He moved her away from him, and kissing her gently on her forehead, he walked out of her office, shaking his head.

"MATT, CALM DOWN. I can't understand what you're saying. And stop swearing—I like to pretend that you don't even know those words." Morgan held the phone with a death grip. Something was wrong at home. Maybe very wrong. Matt never called for help—he preferred to make a terrible mess of things before listening to anyone else's ideas.

"What's wrong with the video recorder? No, I didn't take it anywhere. I left the house before you did this morning, remember? Matt, how can it be gone?" Robbed—they had been robbed? He had to be wrong. "Are you sure? Matt, how about my computer? Well, go check it now." Her computer. If they took it, she would be in a mess, but if they had gotten into her storage disks, she was dead. *Please*, she begged, *not my computer.* "It is? Are you sure? Thank God. Look, Matt, I'm coming home now, but your sister will beat me there. Please don't get her into a panic. You know how she gets. Okay. Thank you, baby. I'll be right there. Yes, I know it's snowing. I'll drive very carefully. Yes, Matt, I'll wear my seat belt. See you in a minute."

"LOOK, KIDS, I just met the man the other day. I can't call him up and ask him to do that," Morgan argued to the youngsters watching her accusingly from the other side of the table. Her kids fought like cats and dogs until they found a common adversary, then they pulled together like a pack of wolves and moved in for the kill.

"You told us he's a cop. Mom. It's his job," Matt said.

"If he doesn't want to, he can always say no. You're the one who keeps saying that it never hurts to try," Steven tried to reason with her.

"I also tell you to clean your rooms. How come you never remember that?" She tried the time-honored diversionary tactic long favored by parents. She never should have told them what Trace did for a living. She knew better than to arm them with knowledge. She couldn't even begin to count how many times she'd wished she'd never let them learn to talk when they were babies. It was only that being a cop was such a glamorous thing to a kid that she'd thought that they'd get a thrill out of knowing that they'd shared pizza with a real live detective.

"Good thing we didn't. Who knows what else they would have taken. Your room was clean and they got your money and radio. My radio is a lot better than yours, and Steven's room is Fort Knox, but they couldn't find our stuff," Matt pointed out in that way that always made her want to do him bodily harm.

"Mom, you're changing the subject. Go call him now, or else go call Daddy," Amanda demanded as if she was accustomed to giving orders and having them followed without hesitation.

"I'm not calling your father, and I can't call Mr. Standon because I don't have his phone number and it's not in the book. You looked—remember?" She didn't think for a minute that a little detail like a phone number would slow her group down for long, but she needed a bit of time. When they pulled Simon into this, they had called in the heavy artillery.

"Call him at the police station. They know his number. If they won't give it to you, then we'll think of something else. But, Mom, you have to ask for it real nice. Okay?"

Good old reasonable hustler Steven was the one who finally backed her into a corner. Sometimes she wondered if they planned these scenes. They did have a point, though. This was really scary, and none of them would get much sleep tonight if she didn't do something. It figured that C.J. would be busy the one time they really wanted him to spend the night. What good did it do to have a little brother if he wasn't at her beck and call, Morgan complained silently as she dialed the phone and worked her way from the switchboard operator to Trace's desk.

"Standon here," the deep voice rumbled over the line.

This situation had all the necessary ingredients to turn into one of those most embarrassing moments in her life. Maybe even worse than when she'd thrown up at her wedding. "This is Morgan Harris, your nutrition instructor?" she said, somehow making it sound like a question.

"Yes, Doctor, I think I remember you."

He was laughing at her. Gripping the phone even more tightly, Morgan glared at the fruit of her womb, who had formed a ring around her, listening to her every word. "You work late—I thought you'd be home by now."

"We public servants are an overworked lot," he answered her solemnly. "You thought I wouldn't be here so you decided to call up and chat?"

"Well, yes," she admitted, as she started to fidget with the phone cord.

"Glad to see you're making your usual sense." His amusement was clearly evident. "So what can I do for you this snowy night, Doctor?"

"We wondered if you wanted to come spend the night." Squeezing her eyes closed, she blurted the question out.

"Who's we?" he asked.

"The kids and I," she muttered, looking bemusedly at the phone cord that was now wrapped around her hand so many times that it was pulling the phone away from her ear.

There was a long pause before he drawled suggestively, "I've never been involved in anything quite that kinky. I'll have to think about it."

"Mom, is he coming? What did he say?" the children asked her at once.

Turning her head away from the phone and holding the mouthpiece against her chest to muffle any noise, she answered them. "No, he can't come. Don't worry, maybe Gramps can come when he gets home," she responded to their crestfallen faces.

"Hold it, lady. I didn't say I wouldn't come. Don't take it on yourself to turn down my dates," he ordered, obviously hearing her. "But just out of curiosity, why do your kids want me over there tonight? They get some clever idea watching their horror flick and now they're looking for a subject?"

"In a way," Morgan told him stiffly, looking longingly at the phone cradle, wishing the phone were resting on it at this very moment. In her next life she certainly hoped she would be a bit more on top of things than she was in this one. "We were burglarized today while we were all at school. A few minutes ago the dog started barking at something in the backyard. I couldn't see anything, but there are tracks in the snow. It kind of looks like someone went from window to window. I guess with the movies and all, we're letting our imaginations run wild. I'm sure it's nothing. Sorry to bother you. Goodbye." Morgan had spoken so quickly that by the time she got to the last few sentences, she was pronouncing them almost as one word.

"Morgan, wait. Don't you dare hang up. How do you know someone went from window to window?" He was no longer amused. In fact, he sounded more coldly professional than she had ever heard him.

"When I went out and followed the tracks, that's where they went. They hadn't filled up with new snow yet, so I could see where to follow him."

"Why did you say 'he'?"

"They were big tracks," she explained simply, sensing that he was getting annoyed.

"Morgan, did it ever enter your mind that leaving your house to traipse after some Peeping Tom might not have been that bright an idea?" he suggested tautly.

"Well, yes, I did get a little nervous when I followed the tracks into the pine trees," she answered sheepishly. It hadn't been as stupid as he was making it seem. After all, she had taken McGee with her. Just because the dog had let someone steal C.J.'s hunting rifle out of the car he was supposed to be guarding didn't necessarily mean that the animal wouldn't defend her. Maybe he was just not materialistic.

"Pine trees," he echoed ominously. "Look, lock the doors and I'll be there in about fifteen minutes. Do not go outside and do not answer the door unless you know it's me."

"Yes, sir." She tried to unwrap the cord from around her hand where it had knotted. "It's snowing hard. I'll open the garage and you can park inside beside my car. Thank you, Trace."

"Morgan—" his voice was very quiet "—you stay in the house. Period. Understand?"

"Yes, Trace, you'll open the garage door yourself. Got it." She wasn't sure if he heard her clearly, as she was talking through clenched teeth, but when he slammed the phone down without harping at her about anything else, she figured he must have gotten the message.

IT WASN'T TEN MINUTES LATER when McGee again started barking by the back door. Soon he had moved into Morgan's bedroom and stood barking at her window. The big black Labrador who was so gentle that his guard dog capabilities had been a family joke was finally proving that he was related to those noble animals who didn't hesitate when it came to defending their people. The eighty-pound animal, with large white teeth exposed in a vicious lip-curling snarl, was showing himself to be a something they definitely wanted on their side.

Watching him, Morgan felt more anxiety than comfort. She wasn't afraid of McGee, but what could possibly be out there that would bring out the killer in their family pet? Glancing at her children, she knew that she wasn't the only one with that thought. Three pairs of fearful eyes kept shifting between the growling dog and the window. It was Matt who finally broke the silence.

"Mom, I'm going into the kitchen to get a knife or something." His voice quavered, but Morgan felt a warm surge of pride at the determined expression in his eyes. What the lanky thirteen-year-old could do against whatever was out there might be debatable, but he didn't lack courage.

"No, Matt, get on the phone in the kitchen. Be ready to call the police if I yell. Do you know the number?" she asked, continuing to watch the closed window curtains that McGee growled at.

"Yes, Mom," he answered, slightly exasperated that she thought he might possibly forget a number.

McGee stopped growling at the window and took off down the hall after Matt, barking aggressively. Passing the boy, he went to the front door and leaped up against it, snarling and growling as if he were going to take the door apart. A moment later the doorbell rang.

Chasing McGee down the hall, Matt was the first one to the door. "Who's there?" he yelled, attempting to make his voice sound low and masculine.

"I don't think they can hear you with McGee and the storm." Morgan had caught up with her son and stood behind him with her hands on his shoulders. "It's probably Trace, but I'm not sure how to tell. Guess we should have gotten one of those peephole things for the door."

"I'll find out." Steven turned from where he stood behind his mother and went back down the hall.

The doorbell rang again, and McGee resumed barking. Steven, Morgan's delicately built son, came back down the hall looking extremely pleased with himself.

"It's him, Mom. I opened the bathroom window a little and looked out. It's him for sure."

"Good work, Steven," Morgan complimented as Matt went to open the door. "Wait, Matt!" she yelled, "let me get hold of McGee."

Calming the growling dog, Morgan watched Trace enter. His size and innate authority were comforting at this particular moment. He wasn't even through the doorway before the kids were telling him that the "Creeper," the name they had instantly given the window peeper, was again out in the yard. Between the dog barking and lunging excitedly and the kids giving him advice on the best way to get into the backyard to shoot the trespasser Morgan could not hear his answer, but it seemed to pacify the children.

Taking off his overcoat and handing it to Steven, Trace walked over to where she held McGee. Holding out his hand to the dog in a gesture of friendship, he spoke over the softly growling dog. "Are you all right?"

"Yes, but what about the guy in the backyard?"

"That was me. I wanted to check things out a little in case someone was still out there." Seeing the question in her eyes he went on. "There's nothing moving out there now. Not even any tracks. The snow's covered them."

"Thank God. I wasn't sure what to do when McGee started barking again. We were just about ready to call the police on you," she joked, hoping her accompanying grin looked less sick than it felt.

"Where did you get the guard dog? I know there were a lot of kids here Friday, but I'm sure I would have noticed him. After all, I'm a trained detective." He smiled gently at her, and she appreciated his effort to lighten the atmosphere.

"My brother had him out hunting, but last Friday you wouldn't have seen this vicious beast, anyway. If McGee had been here he probably would have rolled over on his back to get his belly rubbed. He's never acted like this before." She looked at the dog who was still rumbling low in his throat. Taking Trace's outstretched hand in her own, she brought it closer to McGee, making sure her hand was between the dog and Trace. "Good dog. You're a good dog. It's okay now, McGee," she reassured the dog, who calmed down rapidly. "I'm sorry. I don't know how to call him off you. A lot of sloppy kisses is the only danger he's ever posed to a guest before."

"Don't apologize for him—he was doing a good job. The way he sounded when I was outside your window would have been enough to keep anyone from breaking in." He was petting the dog freely now, and McGee seemed to be slowly melting under his touch.

"Thank you for coming. I tried to get hold of my brother and my dad, but one's working and the other isn't home. We were all a little panicky." She let go of the dog and watched as McGee went through his normal tail-wagging routine.

"All in the line of duty, Teach," he assured her with a flashing grin.

"Sure, I bet. How often does your job entail babysitting?" She was embarrassed and not sure how to act. She'd invited the man to spend the night and now he was here.

"Not that often, but it's kind of nice to be the hero for a change. Normally I don't get much opportunity to do that. But such service is not free. Do you have anything to feed a hungry man for dinner?"

Grateful for the opportunity to do something with herself, she nodded and led the way into the kitchen, feeling a bit like the leader in a parade when the kids all trailed after them. "How come you don't play hero a lot? It seems to me that would be built into your job," she asked conversationally as she started spooning some fish stew left over from their dinner into a bowl.

"I'm with homicide. Generally I get there a little after the fact." The slight ironic grin that had twisted his lip turned into a full-fledged smile as Steven let out a loud, admiring whistle.

"Wow, I bet you see dead bodies all the time. Is it really gross with lots of blood and stuff?" Steven was wide-eyed and looked at Trace with awe. "Do you ever get to go see a body that's been lying around rotting? Do you throw up and stuff? I saw this great movie where the police had to go into an apartment where rats had—"

"Shut up, Steven," Morgan snapped hastily. "That's not dinner conversation, nor should you badger a guest with your sick questions."

"That's okay, Mother." Trace laughed at both her and Steven. "I can handle the bloodthirsty kid's questions. Besides, I thought teachers were supposed to think that there were no such things as bad questions."

"That's 'no such thing as a stupid question,' and it's a lie we tell ourselves to help maintain our sanity."

Morgan looked at her son sternly. "Even if he can tolerate the topic, I can't, so stifle it, Steven."

"Later, mate." Trace winked at the crestfallen boy.

"Hey, Mom, why don't you go work on your book or something. We can entertain Mr. Standon," Matt suggested, looking anything but innocent.

"Enough, boys," Morgan announced in what was clearly to be the last word on the subject.

A COUPLE OF HOURS LATER Morgan looked around at the domestic picture that presented itself to her. Her family had migrated, en masse, to the living room, and around a merrily burning fire, they lay on the floor, totally involved in the game spread out before them. Trace was on the floor with the kids, watching them play and asking questions now and then in an attempt to understand the complexities of an advanced Dungeons and Dragons game.

The scene looked completely natural, as if it were something that happened every day. Even she was comfortable with this man. He had managed to soothe her embarrassment, and he was handling her children so skillfully that she didn't feel the need to run interference. He seemed genuinely interested in the game and questioned the moves they made with sincere respect for their answers. Even the name-calling that arose between the kids on occasion didn't seem to faze him, and she doubted that he was used to hearing people call each other "dragon breath" or "wizard worm."

Simon was always criticizing the way she permitted the kids to quarrel and use the language so innovatively. What he didn't seem to understand was that there were so many things to fight with kids about that you had to pick your subjects carefully or you would be harping at them constantly. The way they fought didn't particularly worry her. They all liked one another, and as long as they weren't using profanities, she didn't mind the language. Besides, how much power did a mother have? She knew lots of families that supposedly did not permit sibling fighting or swearing, and the kids still fought and used awful language.

But Trace seemed to take it all in stride. He had even refused to let Matt involve him in a fight. He hadn't backed down from the teen's rather aggressive challenge. He had just responded as if he hadn't known Matt was trying to start a quarrel. It was basically the same way she handled Matt, but she'd had lots of years of practice and a few parenting classes to help her come up with the technique.

Of course, maybe he did have some experience. When she thought about it, she realized that she didn't know anything about him. He might even have children the ages of hers, for all she knew. She'd assumed that he was single, but having a man kiss you was certainly no guarantee that he didn't have a wife at home.

Lots of married men looked for limited relationships with other women. She'd had a few such men suggest to her that they get together and satisfy mutual human needs, assuring her all the while that what a wife didn't know wouldn't hurt her. But Trace didn't seem that kind. Smiling mockingly at herself, she admitted that she didn't want the hero of the hour turning out to have feet of clay.

"Anyone want some hot cider?" Morgan asked, just to give herself something to do besides think about Trace's wife.

Before anyone could answer, the lights flickered and went out. Almost instantaneously Trace was on his feet, looking out the window.

"They're out all over the neighborhood. The storm must have brought down a line," Trace told them, walking back to the fireplace. He poked the fire, giving them more light.

"Wow," said Matt, looking at Trace with wide, excited eyes. "You thought that someone had turned our power off, didn't you?"

"Well, that thought did cross my mind, but it's not the case." He shot a look of reluctant admiration to the boy, who'd just annihilated any chance he had at covering up his almost instinctive response to the power outage. "Do you have any flashlights, Morgan?"

"Yes, I'll get them." She stood up and started toward the kitchen.

"Wait, I'll go with you," Trace called.

"Do you think there's someone in the kitchen, too?" Amanda asked, wrapping her arms around herself and shivering delicately.

"No, pumpkin, I'm just going to help your mom carry the flashlights," he told her gently.

Feeling her way through the dark kitchen, Morgan called softly to Trace. "Wait there—I'll find the flashlights and shine the light for you."

"Good idea," a deep voice said from right behind her.

"Trace!" Morgan yelped. "You are sneaky. How can you see in here?"

"I can see as well as I need to," he rumbled softly in her ear, as his arms wrapped around her and he pulled her to him until her back rested against his chest. He nuzzled her neck through the thick curtain of hair that fell to her shoulders. "All night I've waited for an opportunity to get you alone. Do you have any idea how hard it is to watch you draped all over the couch looking warm and soft and not be able to even look at you the way I want to?"

"Trace, you said you understood about this being a platonic relationship," Morgan whispered, allowing him to turn her around so she stood facing him in the dark.

"That's tomorrow night when I come over to get the book. Tonight's a different story." His voice was low and husky, and his words were interrupted by little kisses on her jaw and down her neck.

"Did you think I invited you over to sleep with me?" she asked, getting uneasy again. Licking her suddenly dry lips, she tried to think of something to say that would turn the whole thing into a joke.

"Hush, Professor. I know you can't sleep with me tonight. When we make love you're going to concentrate solely on me, not on who might be walking through the door."

He sounded irritated that she had thought he'd misunderstood her, but the lips that unexpectedly covered hers, cutting off any reply she might have made, were soft and gentle.

So nice, so very nice, Morgan thought as her senses started spinning and a strange feeling of weightlessness possessed her. Deliberately moving even closer to him, she used her tongue in the same provocative way that he did, until they were engaging in a sensual game that sent ripples of excitement through her.

A small, high-pitched cry escaped from the back of her throat when Trace pulled her tightly against the hard warmth of his body.

"Oh, lady, what do you do to me?" Trace breathed, gently releasing his hold on her.

Morgan felt as if she'd fall down if he took his support away from her. Dazed, she blurted out the thought that had bothered her half the night. "Are you married?" Embarrassed, she stepped back from him and continued on without giving him the opportunity to answer. "I'm sorry, I didn't mean that. I mean, it's none of my business."

"Hold it, Morgan. My turn to talk." He caught her by her shoulders gently and held her. "No, I am not married, nor have I ever been. And it seems to me that after the few exchanges we've had, you do have the right to ask that question. Or doesn't it make any difference to you?" he added, as if the possibility was an unpleasant afterthought.

"Mom, the flashlights are in the top of the craft cupboard. Can't you find them?" Amanda yelled helpfully from the living room.

"Yes, I think I know where they are now. Thank you, Amanda," Morgan answered her shakily, as she stepped back from Trace and made her way to the cupboard.

Finding the flashlights, she turned one on and carried the others back to Trace. Handing him the extra flashlights, she kept her eyes lowered and answered his question. "Yes, it would make a difference to me. I would hate to think you were that kind of guy." Quickly she walked around him, back to the safety of her living room filled with her children.

3

"MOM, WHERE IS Mr. Standon going to sleep?" Steven asked as they all sat in the darkened living room.

Not willing to risk even a quick peek at the man in question, Morgan replied neutrally, "I thought he could sleep in the Hide-a-bed in the study. I've already made it up."

"Where are you going to sleep, Mom?" Amanda looked up at her mother. "If the electricity is off, the heater on your water bed won't work."

"It won't cool down that quickly. If I get cold, I'll move out here," Morgan replied, patting the couch she sat on.

"Do you think it would be all right if Steven and I brought up our sleeping bags and stayed in the den with Mr. Standon?" Matt asked his mother. "Steven's kind of worried about sleeping down in the basement with the lights out and all."

They had a three-bedroom house, and the boys had been given the choice of sharing a room upstairs or each having his own room in the basement. They had immediately opted for the basement. C.J. had put in a bathroom, a rec room, two bedrooms, and the boys had lived in their own domain ever since. They loved it, except when the electricity was off, which was a fairly common occurrence with Michigan winters.

"I don't think there is room for all of you in the den. Why don't you lay out your bags in the living room?" Morgan suggested, still refusing to look at Trace. Immature as it was, this talk about where they were going to sleep unnerved her. She hoped that by the time she took her South Seas cruise she would be a bit more blasé about such things, but now all she could think about was the fact that Trace couldn't possibly have any pajamas with him.

"We could squeeze up. We wouldn't mind, Mom," Steven suggested hopefully.

"It's fine with me if the boys and I share a room," Trace added, clearly amused.

Risking a quick glance at him, Morgan knew the source of his entertainment was herself. "Wherever you all want to sleep is fine with me, as long as Mr. Standon doesn't mind."

"In that case, I've always kind of wanted to sleep in a water bed," the large man teased seductively, his laughter barely contained.

"Sure, if that's what you want. You three can take my water bed and I'll sleep in the study," Morgan agreed readily, goaded by his laughter into seeking revenge.

"Mom, everyone else gets to sleep with someone," Amanda complained. "Can I sleep with you? It will be icky by myself with the Creeper right outside my window."

"If anyone is still out there he's frozen solid by now, hon. I don't think you need to worry," Trace assured her.

"Ugh, that's even grosser—a dead man right outside my window. His face is probably all twisted up in eternal agony. His hands are reaching out for the lock on my window in a desperate last attempt to gain a bit of life-saving warmth. Warmth that, in the end, was denied him." Amanda delivered her lines with outstretched arms and quavering voice.

Trace replied in a carefully controlled tone, "I never quite thought of it like that."

Looking at his astonished face, Morgan couldn't help herself—she snickered. "Welcome to the Harris House of Dramatic Study. We have programs every Monday and Wednesday nights for your viewing pleasure." Smiling at her daughter she said, "If the boys are going to share the bed with Mr. Standon, then I think it's only fair that we double up, too."

"Great." Steven gave a modified rebel yell. "You're going to love it," he confided in Trace. "Every time someone wiggles, even a little bit, it feels like you're on a boat going over mile-high waves. Matt wiggles all night long, too." Casting his brother a thoughtful look, he added, "You can sleep in the middle, Mr. Standon. You're so big Matt can't push you out of bed."

"Sounds wonderful, Steven," Trace said dryly as he gave the smug-looking Morgan a glance that promised retaliation.

STEVEN HADN'T BEEN JOKING, Trace told himself as he shoved Matt back to his own portion of the king-size water bed. When he'd agreed to spend the night he hadn't seriously considered sleeping with Morgan, but he certainly hadn't planned on this, either.

Actually, he'd come over without giving a thought to the sleeping arrangements. When Morgan had called he had been able to hear, through her embarrassment, fear. It had been that fear that had had him jumping up from his desk and galloping to her rescue like a white knight.

Lord knows why. He'd certainly talked with frightened women before and he'd never felt the need to comfort them in person. There was something about this lady that touched him. The prim, proper, uptight professor, who looked like a strong wind would carry her away, had gotten under his skin. When his frustration with her cool arrogance had goaded him into picking on her a little, and she had overreacted with terror, he'd felt like a fool. It was a role he hadn't found himself in since adolescence, and he had been a little ashamed of himself, especially when she'd gotten sick.

That was the reason he had brought her the pizza—sort of an apology. At least that was the reason he gave himself, but he rather suspected that even then he'd been attracted to her.

The sloppy-looking woman in old jeans and a faded sweatshirt who'd answered the door the other night had startled him. He was a pretty good judge of character—he had to be in his job—but he never would have predicted the changes this lady had gone through.

The proper professor had disappeared, and in her place was a woman who had kids crawling all over her, and who didn't seem to know how to sit in any position other than a sprawl. He liked this lady who laughed, teased and drifted around in her chaotic home as if she was a bit bewildered by it all but was willing to give it her disorganized best. He liked her a lot.

It hadn't been only the woman that left him a bit befuddled, either. His own protective, even somewhat possessive, anger at her total lack of caution when she had flung open the door, had surprised him. He could have been anyone. This town wasn't all that rough, but it was rough enough to justify a homicide division. Her impulsiveness still made his blood run a little cold when he thought about it. Of course, his blood had heated up just fine tonight when he'd discovered the dead bolt on her door had been put in wrong. He would have jumped down her throat if the kids hadn't been watching, but they were already upset enough without listening to him rip into their mother.

Something was going on between this woman and himself that needed exploring. Physically they were hot. All they had to do was kiss and he felt the blood rushing to his head. Morgan was feeling something, too—he was sure of it. When she'd responded to his kiss on the couch, he'd thought that maybe she was a current model of the ever-popular hot divorcée. Since then, he'd come to realize that she was too shy with him to have had much experience. As long as he kept things brotherly she was fine, but as soon as he made her aware of his desire she became very antsy.

Her kids were something else, too, he thought as he gave Matt another shove. They seemed like nice kids, if you liked kids. They created in her house a kind of good-natured free-for-all. It was so different from the way he'd grown up that he'd found himself watching her family, feeling like a foreign visitor watching American television for the first time—amused but a little confused. They didn't exactly talk back to their mother, but they came very close to it. Especially Matt. He saw a lot of himself in the lanky kid's half-angry challenge to the world. If anyone wanted a fight, Matt would be the one to give it to him. Until he grew up a little, he would probably be going out of his way to start a few, too.

Yes, he saw a lot of himself in Matt, but there was nothing similar in the way Morgan handled the kid and the way his parents had dealt with him. Then again, Morgan had nothing in common with the unstable woman who had never been able to look after him properly and who moaned constantly about his father's walking out. By the time Trace was Matt's age, he wasn't home enough that her immaturity had mattered much. Matt, who was active and aggressive even in his sleep, had no idea how lucky he was to be in a family that seemed to see through his bluster and love him.

Hanging around her family had been quite an experience for him. He wasn't sure he wanted to do it a lot but he'd enjoyed himself tonight. It beat sitting around his empty apartment working up some enthusiasm for the studying he had to do. This semester had been a total bust as far as classes went, with the possible exception of the easy home ec course he'd signed up for. Smiling to himself at the absurdity of that choice, he rolled over and tried to ignore Matt pushing against his back.

"BOYS, WAKE UP," Morgan called softly through the bedroom door. It usually took a minor explosion to get the boys up. Whispering through the door was probably nothing more than a lesson in futility, but what else could she do? Trace was in there without pajamas, and the bed, after having Matt sleep in it, probably had even the pillows on the floor.

"Mom, come on in," Steven whispered back to her. "I need your help."

"Is everyone decent?" Morgan whispered back.

"Yes. Come help me with Matt, Mom."

Gathering her courage, Morgan pushed open the door and peeked in. All looked well. Trace and Matt were lying back to back, a blanket twisted around them, dead to the world. They both looked so peaceful and sweet that Morgan couldn't resist just watching them for a moment.

Enjoying the mushy warm maternal glow that always filled her when she watched her children sleeping, and somehow didn't seem all that out of place for Trace, either, she smiled lovingly. Eventually she grabbed Matt's arm and shook him gently, taking care to stay out of reach of his other arm, which had nailed her more than once when she'd wakened him.

"Matt, wake up, honey. Time to get up if you want to eat," she whispered to the stirring boy.

"Okay, Mom, I'm moving," Matt mumbled back at her.

"If that's moving, you're setting a record for the slowest movement ever recorded," his mother teased.

"Actually, I'm going so fast that your eyes aren't able to register any movement," Matt defended himself.

"Up, Matt." Morgan gave him another little shake.

Groaning softly, the dark-haired boy heaved himself off the bed and stumbled blindly out the door after his brother. Left alone with Trace, Morgan took a minute to study the sleeping blonde. Sleep had softened the hard planes of his face, giving him a soft, vulnerable look. No, soft was the wrong word, she mused. He looked softer, but the blatant masculinity and the strength that showed in his face stopped just this side of soft.

Sighing quietly to herself, she started to move away from the bed when a hand grabbed her wrist and pulled her off balance. Stumbling, she fell hard onto the water bed.

"What are you doing?" she demanded of her captor.

"Getting even. Have you ever slept with your eldest child?" Trace had pulled her down so she lay on her back, and he leaned over her, his naked chest holding her in place. "In some circles that would be called cruel and unusual punishment."

"Oh, was he restless last night?" Morgan asked innocently, looking up into the shocking blue eyes a few inches above her and trying to ignore the heat that built up wherever his skin touched her thick terry-cloth robe. "I'm so sorry."

"Why do I find that hard to believe, I wonder?" he growled at her.

"You're in a profession that has made you so skeptical that you don't recognize the truth when you hear it?" she suggested helpfully.

"That could be, or perhaps it was the look of feline satisfaction that lit your face when the boys volunteered to share my bed that raised my suspicions."

"You must be mistaken," Morgan complained in righteous indignation. "I would never so abuse the hero of the evening with such malice aforethought."

"Morgan, you are incorrigible. But lucky for you, I've learned rehabilitation techniques that work with even the hardest cases." He lowered his head and started nibbling on her full lower lip.

The seductive little nips made her whole body tingle and left her hungry for a little more. Lifting her arms up, she wound them around his neck and played with the short hair at the nape of his neck. The slightly abrasive hair, contrasting with the warm smooth skin on his shoulder, sensitized her fingers. Unable or maybe just unwilling to stop, she let her fingers explore his shoulders, moving ever so slowly down his naked back, enjoying the warm firm flesh.

"Hey, lady, I'm supposed to be punishing you. Why are you acting like you're enjoying this?" Trace rumbled in her ear as he continued to occasionally nip her earlobe while tracing it with the warm tip of his tongue.

"Don't know," Morgan sighed. "Maybe I'm just a great actress able to hide even the most excruciating pain."

"If you think this is bad, just wait until I get out the thumbscrews," he threatened. Kissing her ear goodbye, he pulled his head up and looked at her. "Morgan, when we are together like this do you feel something special?"

Suddenly uncomfortable, Morgan tried to wriggle out from under him. "Sure, I feel like I'm going to be specially late for work if I don't get a move on."

"Stop it, Morgan. Enough jokes. Answer my question." The expression in his eyes warned her that he wasn't going to let her off the hook.

"Yes," she whispered, looking at the dense blond hair that covered his unshaven cheeks and made him appear even more masculine.

"Have you ever felt anything like it before?"

"No. It's new to me," she confessed.

"Good. Then we both admit that it's something we should explore further, right?" he demanded.

"I don't think I said that." Morgan stirred under him again.

"Morgan, when was the last time you were with a man?" he asked gently as he lowered his head again and kissed her lips softly.

"I don't think that's a fair question to ask," she charged in a belligerent whisper.

"You're right, it isn't. But you're still going to answer it, because I'm not going to let you up until you do, and eventually someone is going to want to know what happened to their mother."

Glaring up at him, she hissed, "Six years ago, as if it's any of your business."

"When were you divorced?" He didn't seem the least perturbed by her anger.

"Six years ago. Now will you let me up?" Morgan demanded tautly.

Trace exhaled audibly. "Well, that explains why you are so flighty around me, but it doesn't change things. We have something here that would be a shame to waste. Take it from a man who has had a bit more experience in the matter than you've apparently had. So, lady, I give you warning that you'd better be prepared to update your ten-year plan." Noticing the sour expression on her face he smiled. "Don't worry, it will be good for you."

"I've heard that one before."

His face hardened. "The hell you have. Who has been feeding you that line?"

She looked at him in disbelief. "Did you think it was an original?"

His lips twisted in a rueful grin. "No, I suppose not. It just irritated me that someone tried to talk you into bed." Catching her look of amazement he added, "Did I say it made any sense? But tell you what, I'll make you a deal. You don't complain about my illogical jealousies and I won't mention the dead bolt on your front door."

"Oh, the dead bolt," Morgan repeated weakly. "Okay, it's a deal, but that doesn't mean I'm agreeing to anything else."

"We'll see, we'll see," he replied gently. "Now, unless you want to see me in my shorts, you'd better leave. I wouldn't mind you staying, but I thought we might take this gradually. All right?"

"What are we taking gradually?" Morgan questioned suspiciously.

"Your seduction, of course," he drawled suggestively.

When he finally let her wriggle out from under him, Morgan walked stiffly out of the room, refusing to acknowledge his quiet laughter.

MORGAN LOOKED DOWN at the papers in front of her with disgust. Granted this research proposal she was supposedly reviewing wasn't her cup of tea. She preferred human subjects and considerably less exacting measurements than this esoteric bit of research. However, scientific format was scientific format and she was generally able to give her colleagues at least a little constructive feedback.

Not today, however. Today all she could concentrate on was one Trace Standon. As irritated as she was with his high-handed questioning this morning, some of what he'd said made sense. Waiting until her kids were grown before she allowed herself any romantic involvements did sound a bit ridiculous when he referred to it as her "ten-year plan." Maybe it was time to let herself explore that male-female facet of life she'd cut herself off from.

She wasn't about to jump into bed with him, regardless of how physically compatible they seemed to be. But maybe she could agree to a few dates, or dinners, or something.

She liked him. She had liked him Friday night when he had been such a good sport about her house being full of kids, and she'd liked him even more last night. Spending the night with them had gone far beyond the call of duty, but he had done it. Done it without any thoughts of having the favor paid back, or at least he hadn't hinted that she should sleep with him out of gratitude. She liked his teasing and she was comfortable with the idea of his being around her kids. She also, she admitted, rather liked the way he looked, tasted, smelled and felt when she was pressed next to him.

When he kissed her it was like slipping into a warm bathtub. A total sensual submersion that warmed her, supported her and let her drift along in some idyllic never-never land. If a few dates did turn into more, she wouldn't fight it. The voice of vast experience might be right—it might be too good a thing to pass up.

Content with replacing her South Seas cruise with getting to know the flesh-and-blood detective flunking her class, she forced herself back to work.

"HEY, PROFESSOR, how's it going?" A deep voice broke her concentration.

"Good enough. How about yourself? Did you stop by to pick up the book that you forgot again?" She emphasized the "again."

Slapping the heel of his hand to his forehead, he looked at her with laughing eyes. "The book. How could I have forgotten the book."

"Taking lessons from Amanda, I see," Morgan commented in her professorial voice.

"I know a good thing when I see it, and I'm not above stealing from the best," he answered her condescendingly. "However, surprising as this might be, I didn't drop by to amaze you with my thirst for nutritional knowledge." His voice lost its teasing tone, becoming serious. "Are you and the kids going to be all right alone tonight? I'm working until midnight or so, but I could drop by later, if you wanted."

Flustered, Morgan looked down at her desk top. "Thank you, but we'll be okay. It probably wasn't anything sinister, anyway. Besides, I've talked with my little brother, and he's going to come over. He sleeps there half the time already."

"You sure?"

Glancing up, Morgan saw that he was watching her with that intent look that seemed to miss nothing. "Positive. I'm grateful you came over last night. We were all really frightened, and it would have been rough if we'd been alone when the lights went out, but I didn't mean to make us your permanent responsibility. With my brother there, we'll be fine. Anyway," she added teasingly, "do you think you could stand another night listening to my kids insult each other?"

"The verbal abuse doesn't bother me. I picked up a few I can hardly wait to use myself. It's the thought of spending another night within striking range of Matt that makes my blood run cold," he said with a shake of his head. "I think before that kid gets married you should make his bride spend the entire night with him. It would be the only honest thing to do."

Morgan laughingly agreed with him. "When he was little and had a fever, I used to sleep with him so I could keep an eye on his temp. I would always be bruised by morning, and that's when he wore a size-one shoe." Looking at Trace through her eyelashes, she added, "He wears a man's eight now."

"Thanks a lot, lady. There are convicted felons who would be grateful to you for evening up the score with me," he growled at her.

"Poor baby, I should probably give you an extra point or two on your test out of gratitude," Morgan suggested with exaggerated sympathy.

"How many points was I from passing?" Trace asked curiously.

"Twenty-five," she said with a grin.

"Thanks for nothing, Teach," he muttered. Leaning across her desk, he took her chin in his hand, and holding her still, he sprinkled little kisses on her lips.

Frustrated with his teasing, Morgan complained, "How come you won't kiss me the right way?"

"Because when I kiss you the way I want to, it's too hard to stop. You might try to torture me with your fiendish plots, but I refuse to hand you the opportunity," he informed her. Giving her another little kiss, he stood up and started to leave. Halfway out the door he stopped and turned toward her. "By the way, nothing between us is going to be out of gratitude. Not my grades, our relationship, or your body. Understand?"

"I know," Morgan replied, chagrined. "I was only teasing."

"That's what I guessed, but I'm beginning to suspect that you mask quite a bit with your jokes," he explained. "Look, I'll give you a call and we'll get together, okay?"

"Sounds good to me," Morgan answered him shyly.

WHAT A LOUSY NIGHT. It was just as well Morgan hadn't wanted him to drop by. Midnight had turned into dawn before he'd even had time to get tired. Some nights went like that—one thing after another until your regular shift and half of another were eaten up. For some reason he'd thought that his hours would be a bit more regular once he made detective. What a joke!

There were a whole lot of jokes around if you had a certain deviant twist in your thought processes. For example, his so-called partner, Jason, would think it was wildly hysterical that he was freezing his tail off sitting outside Morgan's house. Chances were Morgan wouldn't think it quite so funny, and the way things were going lately, one of the kids would probably decide to go sledding at seven-thirty in the morning and spot him. Maybe he'd better come up with some answers now while he had the time to think.

Let's see. How about, I have your house under surveillance because I'm trying to trap the guy who walked through your backyard two nights ago. I think there's a good chance that he's going to change his tactics and strike at dawn. Probably not a good chance she would buy that one.

Then again, even if she thought he'd flipped, it would be better than the truth. You see, Morgan, the truth is that after spending half the night on a stakeout, listening to my partner talk about how women with kids were only trying to find husbands, I started to get a little suspicious of your story last night. When good old Jason almost burst a gut laughing because, fool that I am, I told him I'd spent the night at your house because you were frightened, it hit too close to my own thoughts, so I defended you a little too gallantly. My partner suggested that my intelligence needed examining if I honestly believed that it was your brother who was spending the night with you tonight.

Once that thought had been planted, it had festered. He kept remembering how nervous and evasive she had been when she'd told him that he didn't need to drop by.

He'd read the lady wrong before—maybe he was off base about a lot of things. No one said she had to be telling the truth about not having lovers. She was a good-looking woman. When he looked at her situation objectively, how realistic was it to assume she had been completely on her own for six years? He'd seen enough of what supposedly "good" people did to know that the chances were pretty slim. So here he was, feeling a hundred times a fool, sitting half a block away from her house watching the front door to see who came out.

He didn't have long to wait before Morgan, dressed for work, opened the garage door. Slipping down in his seat, he watched her drive by with Matt and Steven in the car. When the front door opened, he saw McGee come bounding out through the snow. The large black dog hadn't made it to the street before a man in a T-shirt and jeans stepped out on the porch and called him back.

Trace had to give him credit for something—the dog obeyed him a whole lot better than he did Morgan. He started the engine, slammed his car in gear, and holding himself in tight control, he drove sedately down the quiet residential street.

Damn her. What was her game? Why couldn't she have told him the truth? He could have handled the idea of some competition, but he sure didn't need any involvement with another conniving female. That large-boned, blond, fair-skinned man, running around her house half naked, was about as much her brother as he was.

MORGAN FELT LIKE SKIPPING as she walked down the hall that was filled with bright, chattering students. The man had made only one lecture so far this semester, so she couldn't be the least bit sure that he would make this one. It was just that she wanted to see him so badly that it seemed as if he had to be there. Smiling to herself, she realized that Trace wasn't the only one picking things up from Amanda.

She'd thought about him all last night. Finally when the kids had gone to bed, C.J. wanted to know why she was so preoccupied. She and C.J. had always been close. She was five years older than he was, but often it felt like the two of them against the world. He'd been there for her divorce and the custody hearing, and she was helping him keep his sanity during this trial separation his immature wife had insisted on. She'd told him about Trace. About how she was unsure that a romantic involvement would be good for the kids, and about her own feelings of inadequacy.

C.J. had let her talk herself out, and then in a blunt, brotherly fashion told her she was paranoid. Of course the kids could handle it. After all, she wasn't planning on a different guy for each day of the week. It would be good for them to see a little of the dynamics between a woman and a man. It would be especially good for Matt, who, with his preoccupation with swashbuckling fantasy fiction, had reduced all such relationships to "me master, you slave."

He had been even less sympathetic about her feelings of inadequacy. If she couldn't see that she was a dynamite person, then he wasn't about to tell her.

Brothers were such wonderful people. At least little brothers.

Now she could hardly wait to see Trace and talk with him. She even had a legitimate reason to start a conversation.

Looking around the lecture hall, Morgan took only a moment to find him. He'd moved from the back of the hall into the second row, and because the first row tended to be empty in big lecture halls, there was no one sitting between them. Catching his eye, Morgan smiled openly at him, but instead of returning her smile he just watched her, his face a cold, impregnable mask.

Thrown off balance, Morgan busied herself finding the week's reading assignment and focusing it on the overhead projector. Monday, when she'd thought he was going to shoot her, he'd waved and smiled. Why was he now acting as if he'd never seen her before? The only reason she could come up with was that he was maintaining a professional attitude in public as she had pretty much agreed to seeing him socially.

A few minutes into her lecture, Morgan had to revise her thinking. He wasn't being subtle, he was downright hostile. What could have possibly happened between yesterday, when he'd told her he'd call, and this morning? Refusing to allow the icy shiver that raced down her back to interfere with her lecture, she focused her attention on a group sitting in the center of the hall and directed her remarks for the rest of the hour at those students, who eventually became so unnerved by her continuous attention that they put away the campus newspaper and started taking notes.

At the end of the lecture, Morgan risked another glance at Trace. He was no longer glowering at her. He was smiling and talking with a young female student who sat beside him. Something he said made the woman blush and look up at him with admiring eyes.

Taking courage from his seemingly improved mood, Morgan walked over and stood in front of him.

When he noticed her, his smile was replaced by the indifferent mask. "Yes, Dr. Harris? Is there something you wanted?" he asked coldly.

Wishing she had never walked across to see him, Morgan looked at his forbidding expression and the curious one on the face of the young woman beside him. "If you could see me for a moment after class, I would appreciate it." She'd spoken in what she hoped sounded like the same professional voice she would use to any student.

She walked back to the podium and was reassembling her lecture notes when Trace came over. "You wanted to see me?" he asked, his voice doing nothing to warm the iciness in her suddenly clumsy fingers.

"I just wanted to tell you that we found out the Peeping Tom was one of Matt's friends. Matt's been forbidden to hang around with that particular child, and that's why he was creeping around." She felt as if she were nervously rattling on and on. If she didn't get herself under control soon she'd end up throwing up again.

"Well, that's convenient, isn't it, Dr. Harris?"

Looking into his glacierlike eyes, Morgan swallowed the lump that had formed in her throat. Turning back to her notes, she gathered them up. "That's all I wanted to see you about," she mumbled, keeping her face averted as she pushed by him and blindly left the lecture hall.

Morgan dumped her lecture folders on her desk, and after picking up another stack of folders, carefully locked her office and left the building. It was a twenty-minute walk over to the lab she was using for her research, and she needed every minute of that solitude.

She felt like a raw wound. Everything was hurting and at the same time numb. She'd never dealt well with rejection, and that's what this had to be. Why would a man flirt with you one day and hate you the next? *Hate* didn't feel like too strong a word, either, for the coldness he'd shown toward her.

Maybe Trace was unstable. Maybe, but she honestly didn't think so. It could be that after spending a night thinking about it, he'd decided that she wasn't worth the hassle of a relationship. That was perfectly understandable, but if that had been the case he could have just not called her—he didn't have to carry on the way he had today.

There was always the faster-horses younger-women theme. She'd been taught that one in excruciating detail by her ex-husband. She'd have bought that if he'd been around long enough to get bored with her, but that was hardly the case.

In the long run it didn't really matter. Her euphoria of this morning was just a hollow balloon that had been burst, but life still went on. He was one student out of a class of almost four hundred, and she was his professor. That was the total extent of their relationship. She had been Dr. Harris for a number of years, and since that's the way he apparently wanted to play the game, she would continue to be Dr. Harris with him.

4

"OH, ANN, DON'T. It's hard enough facing that class without knowing that you've been using me as a human Kleenex," Morgan complained to the grinning two-year-old who was rubbing her nose against her shoulder.

This would be the fourth lecture she'd given since the settling in of the ice age. Trace, never missing a lecture, sat in the same seat, looking as friendly as a glacier. At least toward her. To his "groupies," he was all smiles. The mature, masculine look seemed to have a great deal of appeal to a half dozen or so young female students who made it a point to sit close to him and flirt during lectures. It was almost amusing watching the young women maneuver for the seats beside him. Almost.

She still wasn't sure why he felt obliged to give her those hard, icy glares. There was no doubt that it was more than simply a case of losing interest in her. The man seemed to really despise her. The best idea she'd come up with was that perhaps he'd heard something about the charges her ex-husband and his wife had made against her at the custody hearings a couple of years ago. If someone chose to believe that pack of lies, then they'd have reason to hate her. Beyond that, there was nothing dramatic enough in her life to justify the intensity of Trace's dislike.

The thought that Trace believed any of that garbage infuriated her. The judge hadn't believed it, her lawyer had made mincemeat of it, and even Simon had looked as if he had wanted to crawl under a rock toward the end, but apparently Trace had taken it on himself to judge her guilty.

Her anger made it easier to face him three times a week. She no longer avoided looking in his direction. In fact, she made it a point to look directly through him, as haughtily as possible, at least four times during the fifty-minute class. She could hardly wait for the next test. If he did pass it, she promised herself that she was going to personally fold, spindle and mutilate his computer card.

Her attitude of supreme superiority, which she sincerely hoped sat on Trace as comfortably as a bad case of poison oak, was going to be a bit difficult to maintain with the addition of her nieces to the picture. But there was no helping it. C.J.'s erratic wife had unexpectedly dumped the children on her doorstep that morning. Morgan had tried to get hold of C.J., but he was out on the highway cleaning up an accident. The men at his garage had reached him by radio, so he knew she had the girls, but she had not been able to coordinate any plans with him. She hoped he would show up before class, but unless he walked through the door in the next five minutes she was going to have two very young students.

Finding Kelly a seat in the front row, opposite where Trace usually sat, and settling her in with crayons and some computer cards for coloring, Morgan hoisted Ann to her hip and started setting up for her lecture.

TRACE UNCONSCIOUSLY squared his shoulders and pushed open the door to the lecture hall. This whole situation was getting a bit out of hand, and it was his own fault. So she had lied. So she had some other man spend the night. He was hardly her conscience. He'd run into a lot worse behavior from people without having the overriding urge to make them pay for their errors.

He had to give Morgan credit, he thought grudgingly. She hadn't buckled under the pressure he'd exerted. She glared at him as if she were the Queen Mother and he someone of the rabble so far below her that she couldn't even see him.

It was looking as if this situation he had childishly created was going to make him a lot more unhappy than it did Morgan. Jason had laughingly assured him that probably at least a couple of the girls who crowded in around him were of legal age, but he doubted it. He'd first flirted with the child who happened to be sitting beside him in the hopes of getting to Morgan. It hadn't had any effect on her, but he was beginning to feel like a stag being run by dogs.

He could understand young females feeling the need to test out their probably newly discovered sexual power, but this was getting absurd. It was embarrassing to be the object of quite so much blatant adolescent fantasy. At one point last week he'd considered coming on strong to a couple of them and scaring them off, but he'd reconsidered quickly when he'd seen the predatory look in the eyes of some of them. They probably wouldn't run, and then he'd really be in trouble. He had to come up with something, however, and come up with it fast.

Taking his regular seat, he looked toward where Morgan stood getting ready to lecture. Why did she have her niece with her? He had to smile at the awkward picture she made, Old Superprof with a baby slung on one hip. Catching sight of his own personal pack of hunting females, and at the same time noticing Kelly sitting quietly in the front, he was out of his chair and walking over to sit beside the four-year-old. Never let it be said, he told himself, that he was too big a man to hide behind a baby's diapers.

"Hi, sweetheart. Do you remember me?" he asked the shyly smiling child as he sat down beside her.

"Sure, you're Aunt Morgan's boyfriend. Wanna color with me?" Kelly invited. "We have to be real quiet, but we can make pictures to hang in Aunt Morgan's office if we want."

"That sounds like the best offer I've had in a long time." Trace helped himself to a few of the computer cards and a red crayon. "How come you get to watch Aunt Morgan today?"

"My mommy can't stand to be around Ann and me because we're bad," she told him in a forlorn little voice.

"You're not bad, honey." Trace responded to the look of pain that reminded him vividly of Morgan's eyes when he'd snapped at her last week. "Your mom just probably needed to go someplace where children couldn't be with her."

"Aunt Morgan said that Mommy knew that Daddy wanted to see us really bad," Kelly told him solemnly, obviously not believing it.

"I'm sure your daddy does, hon. I wanted to see you and I'm not even your daddy." Feeling totally inadequate, the large man tried to comfort her.

He watched Morgan try to run a class with a baby. This was turning out to be the most interesting lecture so far. For the first few minutes Ann had kept her face hidden against Morgan's shoulder. Shortly however, much to the delight of the students, she started to play peekaboo with the audience. Warmed by her success, she tried to climb out of Morgan's arms, but Morgan refused to oblige her. With rather insightful maliciousness, Ann was now, unbeknownst to her aunt, hard at work on Morgan's blouse buttons.

Trace enjoyed the show until he realized that he wasn't the only one taking an interest in it. In a surprisingly heated rush of possessive outrage, he glanced back at the fascinated class. Morgan's striptease act was supposed to be for him alone. This group of kids had no right to see that triangle of beige bra that peeked through her open blouse.

Pushing himself out of the narrow chair, he walked over to Morgan, who had stopped lecturing and stood looking at him indignantly. What was wrong with the woman? Couldn't she spot the white knight again riding to her rescue?

"Come here, Ann." Trace held out his arms to the baby, who came to him without a fuss.

"What do you think you're doing?" Morgan hissed angrily at him.

"Button your shirt."

She blinked in surprise and looked down at her blouse, which was half unbuttoned. "Oh, my God," she whispered, trying to glance furtively at her class, which was hidden from her view by Trace's broad chest.

"Exactly." Trace shielded her until she had regained her modesty.

With Ann still in his arms, he turned and walked back to his seat. He was almost ready to sit down when the class realized what he had done and, acting as one, booed.

Trying to sidetrack Ann from his gun, which she had inadvertently discovered and was fascinated with, Trace didn't notice the large blond man until he heard the soft voice.

"Kelly, are you and your sister ready to go? We get to ride in the tow truck today." The familiar-looking man kneeled in front of Kelly.

"Daddy!" Kelly whispered delightedly. At the same time, the warm little bundle in his lap exploded into a wriggling creature determined to escape.

Laughing quietly, their father nodded to a grim-looking Trace, who had just recalled where he'd seen the man before. Taking his youngest daughter in his arms, C.J. kissed Kelly on top of her head.

C.J. was gathering up his children's paraphernalia, about to slip quietly out of the class, when Morgan put a chart on the overhead projector and told the class to copy it.

Walking over, she spoke quietly to her brother. "You're drenched. You'd better get out of those wet clothes before you get sick."

"Yes, Mother." He grinned at her briefly before his face took on a bleak look. "Morgan, I'm really sorry. I had no idea that she was going to dump them on you like this."

"Don't worry about it," she said, dismissing his concern. "It's better that you know where the kids are likely to be if she's going to pull this stunt often. Do you have any plans for them today?"

"Yeah, I finally got a hold of Mom. She's going to watch them until I get off tonight."

"Poor Mom," Morgan smiled fondly. "First she raises my kids and now yours."

"It's okay. That's what mothers are for."

"Watch it, baby brother—you're talking to a mom," Morgan warned.

"Come on, Morgan, you know you want Matt dependent on you until he's thirty," he teased.

"Leave, C.J., while you can still walk," she growled, shooting Trace a cold look before returning to the podium.

FOR A FEW HOURS Morgan toyed now and then with the idea of adopting a more mature attitude to Trace's behavior. There was probably no point in glaring at him every chance she got. And after all he had saved her from a great deal of embarrassment by stopping Ann's little show.

Still operating under a slight feeling of gratitude toward the man, Morgan walked down the stairs to her graduate seminar behind a group of well-dressed attractive female students. Hoping her ears weren't growing from the effort she was making trying to eavesdrop, she listened with interest. It seemed that she hadn't been the only one Ann had uncovered in class this morning. Trace's shoulder holster had been noticed by at least one of his groupies, and the fact that the man wore a gun made him one intriguing mystery. Speculation regarding his profession ran from spy to CIA member to mafia hit man. The conversation that really interested Morgan was the one about the bet. A few of her students had a twenty-five dollar bet going on who would be the first to date Trace. If the date ended up in Trace's bed, the payoff was upped to one hundred dollars.

Trying to decide whether she was shocked, jealous or amused, Morgan did not notice that the topic of discussion was walking down the hall until he put his arm around her and kissed her cheek.

"Hello, sweetheart," he greeted the stunned woman, whose sense of gratitude was instantly replaced by suspicion. "What—" was as much as Morgan was able to sputter before he interrupted her.

"I'm glad you made it to work this morning. You looked so comfortable in bed that I didn't think you'd get up." He smiled a knowing lover's smile and added seductively, "Lord knows you had reason to be tired after last night. Morning, ladies," he said brightly, nodding to the young women who stood watching him with great interest as he bodily moved a rigid Morgan toward the lecture hall.

"What do you think you're doing?" Morgan whispered angrily, pushing his arm.

"Walking you to class, love. And here you are, safely delivered." He gave her a little push to the speaker's podium and, turning, rushed away.

SHE WOULD KILL HIM. Gun or no gun, the man was dead meat. Her cheeks flushed with rage. She'd never forget the way her department head had avoided any eye contact with her while the woman had delivered her "little talk" about professional conduct regarding students of the opposite sex. Trace's life was over. Only the minor detail of carrying out the act remained.

No one had the right to do what he had done to her. First he'd used his kisses to awaken a sensuality that she'd almost forgotten about. Then, for no good reason, he'd pulverized her self-confidence by dropping a ton of rejection on her. And then, like adding a cherry to the top of a sundae, he'd played the part of being on intimate terms with her and had landed her in hot water. He might not know it but he was, at that very moment, one of the living dead.

She had never been so humiliated in her life. She clenched her gloved fists and kicked viciously at another pile of snow. How could she face any of them again? Sure, theoretically only the department head knew about the incident, but she knew how fast gossip traveled around the place. Already the department's Romeo had taken it on himself to suggest she keep things more discreet in the future. He had even offered to give her some tips on managing a student seduction. Thank God it was Thursday. Only one more day and then she'd have a whole weekend to hide.

A new wave of rage turned Morgan off the path and had her forging her way aggressively through a foot of new snow. The snow would have to get a lot higher before she would be able to burn off her anger in the short walk to her lab. At the rate she was going, she would reach her lab and still have to walk around the building a half dozen times before she'd be able to talk civilly to the high school students who were the guinea pigs in her current study.

"Morgan," a voice called out behind her. "Morgan, wait up."

Recognizing the voice, she picked up her pace. Dead, that's what he was going to be. *Dead meat, dead meat, dead meat,* she chanted to herself as she stomped more forcefully through the snow.

"Morgan, I said wait," Trace caught her arm and spun her around until she faced him.

"Don't touch me and don't you dare try to talk to me, you refugee from a cesspool," Morgan told him stiffly.

"Hey, come on. I know it was a mean trick, but I had to do something to get those Junior League femmes fatales off my tail. No harm was done. What the heck, it probably helped your image."

Calming her down had been a hopeless cause to begin with, but the little smile that hovered about his mouth was Morgan's breaking point.

"No harm done. No harm done, he tells me. Look, worm belly." Morgan started poking a gloved finger into his chest. "I have just gotten out from a little talk with my department head. She felt the need to remind me that in my position I have a certain authority over students that makes it essential that I in no way abuse the trust that parents put in the university when they send their little darlings here."

"What are you talking about?" the suddenly serious man asked, grasping her hand.

"I'm talking about the poor distraught student who went in and complained about how I seduced her boyfriend. I'm talking about some overgrown buffoon who announced to the world that he had spent the night with me. And, last but not least, I'm talking about the poor innocent student I intimidated with my formidable authority into thinking that he had to share my bed." Morgan, unable to control her frustration any longer, kicked Trace in the shins. "You know the young man, don't you? He's the one who's about to be shot with his own gun."

Wincing from the force of her kick reinforced by her heavy snow boots, Trace grated harshly, "Morgan, did you explain to them that I was hardly an eighteen-year-old boy?"

"Of course not. I didn't want them to link your murder up with me. I wasn't given the chance to defend myself. I was just warned that the department frowned on such behavior. 'Dear, I'm sure we don't need to discuss this awkward situation any longer,'" Morgan mimicked her boss. Her fury growing as she relived the patronizing, humiliating scene, Morgan tried to kick Trace a second time. Unfortunately Trace had, without her noticing, moved out of reach, and kicking into the air, Morgan lost her balance and fell backward in the snow.

"I'll help you up if you promise to stop kicking me," Trace offered as he stood over her, his eyes reflecting no hint of humor or amusement.

From this position he did seem rather formidable, Morgan thought, looking up at the grim man. Maybe kicking him wasn't such a hot idea. She should probably just go for his gun without giving him any warning. "I don't make promises to pig droppings," she told him loftily while she scrambled to her feet.

"I'm beginning to see where your kids picked up their unique vocabulary," he said dryly, as he caught her elbows and supported her in the slippery snow.

"I learned it from them," Morgan snapped nastily, brushing the snow, and his arm, off her coat. "And I've never had call to use it on anyone but my brother up until now. If you will excuse me, I still have a job to do. No thanks to you."

"I'll walk you," he said flatly, catching a little firmer hold of her arm.

"Don't bother." Morgan tried to pull her arm out of his grip.

"No bother."

"I don't want your company, Trace."

"Fancy that. I never would have guessed," he retorted sarcastically as he pulled her along with him.

With dignity, that's how she would conduct herself—with silent dignity, Morgan swore as she stumbled along beside him in the snow. Actually, after venting her anger on him, she wasn't that mad anymore, but she'd be hanged if she would let him know it. He had no idea his outrageous comments would get her into trouble, and she'd bet he was surprised, and not particularly overjoyed, that someone in the class had considered him her boyfriend.

Although not happy with the way he had done it, she was pleased that he had felt the need to stifle the interest of his classmates. The thought that one of the young women might actually collect that hundred dollars had not sat well. Her experience with men was not extensive, but she was well aware that lots of men found teenagers very attractive. She'd been only nineteen when Simon, who was thirty-three, had successfully maneuvered her into marriage.

"What kind of research do you do in here?" Trace nodded his head toward the large sports complex they were walking up to.

Not sure she was entirely willing to let him off the hook that easily, Morgan considered ignoring his question. On the other hand, even that fleeting comparison she'd made between Trace and her ex-husband made Trace look good. Of course, a rattlesnake would look good compared to Simon.

"Morgan, I'm sorry I got you in a mess, but how long do you plan on pouting?" he asked, a little frustrated.

"About as long as your shin hurts," she answered, giving up her attempt to stay angry. "I'm looking at teenager's perceptions of their own bodies." When he looked questioningly at her, she went on. "I have kids that are classified obese, overweight, average and underweight. We take a picture of them in a bathing suit, and then put the picture in a machine that allows you to adjust the image, making the person appear to look fatter or slimmer." Warming to her subject, she slipped into her professorial tone. "We distort the picture and then ask the subject to adjust the focus until the image is a correct reflection of what they think they really look like. We then compare and see if the teens self-image is a true reflection of reality. We're trying to establish some statistical relationship between body weight and perceived body image. We hope we'll be able to draw some correlations that will give us a little better understanding of the unconscious drive behind the anorexic, and some ideas on motivational problems occurring with the extremely overweight."

"Morgan, my shin still hurts," Trace muttered.

Fighting back a smile, she asked, "With your burning desire to learn all there is to know about nutritional concerns, how is it you happen to be taking a freshman nutrition course?"

"Oh, I was assured by my adviser that it was the easiest way to pick up the four credits that I found out at the last minute I needed to graduate this term." Trace shook his head ruefully. "I should have guessed that any adviser who managed to compute my credits wrong in the first place would give dumb advice."

Stopping in front of an office door, Morgan turned to him. "You can't go any farther than this. If you think the kids in class made it rough on you, you'd never survive my high school group."

"Morgan, have dinner with me tonight." Trace laid his hand on her shoulder, his eyes never leaving hers.

Astonished, she looked up at him. The man was weak in the head. For almost two weeks he had done his best to freeze her over with his iceman treatment, and now, after practically ruining her reputation, he wanted to take her out? Even if she had been tempted, and under oath she would have to admit that he still looked very good to her, her ego wouldn't let her risk another rejection. She would need a few successes with men before she would have the courage to take this one on again. He'd have to wait until she got back from her cruise. "No, thank you," she answered, looking him squarely in the eyes, before turning to enter the human performance lab.

MORGAN WALKED OVER to answer the front door at the same time that she snapped at her boys. "If you two are going to continually fight with each other, please go back down in the basement and spare us your lousy dispositions." They'd been at it for two weeks, and she'd had it.

"What are you doing here?" she snapped at the man who stood in her doorway in much the same tone she'd used with the boys.

"I came to get the book you said I could use." Trace stood at her door casually, as if dropping by her house was a natural everyday occurrence.

"Sorry, I lost it." She tried to close the door, only to have him block it with the palm of his hand as he walked by her.

"Then we'll just have to go over the lectures I missed." He looked around her house appraisingly as he closed the door behind him. "What are the boys fighting about?"

"Nothing. I did not invite you in," she reminded him, crossing her arms in front of her and staring at him belligerently.

"They must be fighting about something. I heard you yelling at them through the door." He took off his overcoat and hung it in the entry closet.

"So go report it to Protective Services," Morgan seethed between clenched teeth. Invite the man to spend one night and he thought he lived there.

Her reference to the agency that dealt with child abuse cases earned her a curious glance from Trace, but no more. He walked by her into the doorway of the family room and silently stood watching the boys bicker. Refusing to let him take over her house completely, Morgan stomped after him.

"That's a fight if I ever heard one. Why don't you tell me what it's about before I feel compelled, as a peace officer, to stop it." Trace smiled into her hostile eyes.

"You stay out of it. It's got nothing to do with you." Morgan moved around him so she stood between him and the boys.

"I didn't think it did. Who's it got to do with?" he asked in a deceptively mild voice that, she knew instinctively, meant he would not give up.

"Steven wants Matt to spend Saturday with their father," Morgan hissed up at the man who was infuriating her.

"Why doesn't Matt want to see his dad?"

"He doesn't like him." Could you call a cop to have a cop kicked out of your house? Probably not.

"Why?"

"He lectures him. Why don't you leave? I'll find the book and you can pick it up after class next week."

Casting a look that seemed to suggest that she could do better than that, he asked, "What does the kids' father do for a living?"

"He's a professor of philosophy," she replied irritably.

Trace whistled softly under his breath. "Poor Matt. Why does Steven want Matt to see him?"

Reading determination in his blue eyes, Morgan gave up. Maybe she would tell him, he would see that she was the terrible mother she'd been accused of being, and then he'd leave. "It is absolutely none of your business, but Steven wants Matt to go with him because the boys' father and Matt always fight, and thus a Saturday morning outing lasts only an hour. My insurance on the house is a $250 deductible, which is just about what a VCR costs. So Steven wants to see his father because he wants to hustle him into replacing the VCR that was taken."

Morgan started counting off the preordained chain of events on her fingers, "Steven will call up Simon and lay some story on him about how they miss him. Simon, feeling guilty because he generally ignores the boys, will agree to spend all day Saturday with them. He'll pick them up at quarter to ten, right before the stores open. He and Matt will be ready to kill each other by ten-ten. Steven will suggest they go to a store, and Simon will jump at the chance to alleviate his ever-growing guilt by playing Santa. Since the stores will have just opened and be almost empty, they will be able to buy the VCR that Steven has already picked out. The boys and the VCR will be home before eleven."

Looking a little stunned, Trace asked, "Do they pull this number often?"

"No, it takes a whole lot of work, and frequently a few bruises from Steven to get Matt to spend even an hour with his father. There are not many things that are worth that much of Steven's effort."

"Lady, I know successful con men who are not as polished as your kids. Does it make you nervous living with them?" he asked, looking over her shoulder with new respect at the boys who were glaring at each other.

"Yes." *But not nearly as nervous as you do*, she added silently. "What are you doing here?"

"Is that popcorn I smell?" He looked around hopefully.

"Yes," she answered shortly.

"Aren't you going to offer me any?"

"No, and that fake hangdog look isn't going to get you anywhere, either."

"Hey, Steven, is there any popcorn left?" Trace called over her head.

"Sure, there's some in the bag on the counter." The angel-faced boy brightened up as he gestured toward the kitchen.

"Thanks." Putting his hands on her shoulders, Trace moved her out of his way and walked into the combined kitchen–family room. Helping himself to a bowl of popcorn, he joined the boys, not bothering to glance in her direction even once.

SLUMPING DOWN LOWER into her chair, Morgan tried to come up with some way of getting one large man out of her family room and into the cold outdoors. She had done her utmost to freeze him out, but her best effort hadn't succeeded in making him even a tiny bit uncomfortable. Of course, there was no real reason that he should even notice her with the kids going out of their way to entertain him.

The boys had stopped fighting with each other and had started soliciting Trace's opinion on everything from whether women would be happier if they were the slaves of "real men"—she was going to burn Matt's barbarian book and poster collection—to how much blood could pour out of a person after his heart had stopped beating, compliments of Steven. Amanda had gotten into the act, and in tights and a leotard, had put on her own modern dance recital complete with dramatic poses and giggles.

Why should the man even notice her cold shoulder? He probably had never been so catered to. Amanda had even made him a sandwich when she'd discovered he'd come straight from work without eating.

She'd had high hopes for a minute there when Matt had asked Trace's help with a math assignment, but even that had fizzled. After taking one look at the math problem, Trace had announced, without the slightest hesitancy or embarrassment, that it was beyond him. Whether Trace knew it or not, that admission had raised him about as high as an adult could go in Matt's books. Narrowing her eyes suspiciously at Trace, she decided that either the man had a whole lot of smarts when it came to kids or someone had briefed him about Matt.

She'd about given up hope of getting everyone to bed at a decent hour when Trace stood up and announced that he'd better be going. Morgan cringed when Amanda asked him to come over the next night for dinner. Friday was her night to cook, and she would like him to taste her special spaghetti. Morgan knew her cause was lost when neither of the boys asked Amanda what was so special about a jar of sauce from the store dumped on some noodles. Resigning herself to company for dinner, she was surprised at the little disappointed lurch her heart made when he politely turned Amanda down, saying he had other plans. After that, it wasn't the least bit hard to glare angrily at him when he offhandedly said goodbye to her.

THANK GOODNESS it was the end of the week, Morgan thought as she got into her car to go home. All her weeks were a bit hectic, but usually only her home life drove her crazy. Work was generally an oasis of organization. Not lately, however. With the aggravation she'd experienced because of Trace, her nieces and her department head, she was looking forward to the weekend the way she sometimes longed for Mondays.

To give Trace the credit due him, he had managed to rebuild her credibility with the department. Morgan smiled to herself as she tried to visualize what had gone on between the head of her department and Trace before Trace had insisted she be called in for the impromptu meeting. He must have put on quite an act.

Apparently he'd even managed to subtly let his jacket fall open so they'd been able to see his gun. Grinning, Morgan wondered whether that had been before or after he'd told them he was a homicide detective. The man had a talent that put Amanda to shame.

Watching the hard, dangerous-looking man snap questions to her boss, Morgan could easily visualize him reducing murderers to little puddles of jelly. When the unscheduled meeting ended, Morgan was being privately warned to be very careful—she was a nice young woman and the man was far out of her league.

Her department head asked what kind of grades Trace was earning and had actually cringed when

Morgan answered. The woman hadn't come right out and told Morgan to pass him regardless, but she had suggested that some older students, who were holding down responsible positions in the community, sometimes needed a little extra consideration. Morgan had the sneaking suspicion that she would approve of any grade just as long as it kept that man out of her office.

Morgan laughed out loud. She had to admit that Simon was probably right—her sense of humor was too immature to fit well into an academic environment. She had loved Trace's whole performance. While Trace sat across from her, looking as if he ate nails for breakfast, she had slipped off one of her shoes and, under the table, had gently kicked the shin that was bruised from the day before. Unless she was way off, the especially grim look that had crossed his face was nothing more than an attempt to control a smile. She did like the man; it was too bad that nothing could come of that fondness.

"Hells bells," Morgan groaned as she noticed the flashing red light in her rearview mirror. Ten to one she hadn't come to a complete stop at that corner again. This would be her second ticket this year for the same thing. She'd get one, too. You always heard about people talking their way out of tickets, but she rather suspected those stories fell into the same category of wishful thinking as those of people claiming to make expenses when they went gambling.

Pulling the car over to the curb, Morgan felt her last hope desert her when the patrol car followed. She dug out her license, registration and proof of insurance as she waited in resignation for the officer to approach her car.

"Ma'am, would you please step out of your car," the young man directed her.

Glancing at him in surprise, she did as he'd requested. "Do you want to see my license?" she asked the nervous-looking kid. It must be a sign of advancing age when you wondered if your authority figures shaved, she thought with a flash of grim humor.

Maybe it was his first ticket and he didn't yet know what he was supposed to do. Feeling maternal toward the agitated kid, she decided that she would help him out. After all, one of these days her kids would be out making a mess of their first jobs.

"Please put your hands on the car roof," he ordered nervously.

Turning around and following his request, Morgan explained kindly, "You're just supposed to look at my licence, registration and proof of insurance. Then you go call someone to make sure I'm not a criminal, give me a ticket and remind me to drive safely."

"Yes, ma'am. I'm afraid it's a little more complicated than that," he explained, slipping up behind her, reaching for her hands and snapping a pair of handcuffs on her.

Spinning around to face him, Morgan lost all maternal feelings as she looked at her shackled wrist. "Just what do you think you are doing? You're making a horrible mistake. Who do you think I am?"

"Dr. Morgan Harris," the uniformed man answered, much to her shocked surprise.

"Well, what are you arresting me for?" she asked, getting more confused by the minute.

"Threatening a police officer," he mumbled, shifting uncomfortably under her hard stare.

"Is this officer by any chance named Trace Standon?" Morgan drawled, deceptively calm.

"Yes, ma'am."

"In that case, you had better take me in because I am going to kill that slug before he has a chance to crawl back under his rock," she snarled at the man who was looking around a little frantically.

"Thank you, I'll take it from here," an instantly recognizable voice said from the other side of her car.

"Good. Great," the young man replied in relief. Turning, he beat a hasty retreat to his car.

"You shouldn't have sent your reinforcements away quite so soon. I have the feeling you're going to need them," Morgan told Trace as he walked toward her.

Ignoring her, Trace opened her car door, took out her keys and proceeded to lock her car up.

"What do you think you're doing?" Morgan glared at him as he stood watching her with his vivid sky-blue eyes laughing at her.

"Taking you out for dinner." He moved forward quickly and kissed her lips.

"Wanna bet?"

"Yep." He grabbed her shackled wrist and pulled her toward his car, which he had parked behind his cohort in crime.

5

TURNING IN to the parking lot of a Chinese restaurant, Trace looked over at his scowling, silent companion. "Have you decided to cooperate with me yet?"

"Sure, just as soon as the first pig flies by," Morgan retorted. She was leaning against the car door in an attempt to keep as much distance between them as she could manage.

The relaxed, broad-shouldered man smiled at her. Reaching over, he caught hold of her shackled hands and dragged her along the seat until she was beside him. "You have such a charming way with words," he commented, unlocking one of the cuffs. "And to think that one of the things that worried me about going back to school was whether I could take dealing with pompous, overeducated instructors."

Morgan's newly born hope for an easy escape was crushed when, as he freed one wrist, he locked the cuff to the steering wheel. "You can't do this, you know. My kids are expecting me at home," she reasoned as she studied the handcuff. It was really kind of clever the way they made them to fit any size wrist. With a little imagination she could come up with all sorts of uses for it. Maybe she could talk Trace into letting her try one out as a child restraint. She could lock Matt to McGee until the dog was fed and watered, or even Trace to her nutrition book.

"No, they aren't. I called your house before I had you picked up and they know we're on a date." Choosing to pretend he hadn't heard her unladylike snort at his reference to a date, he went on, "In fact, your brother was there and he said he was spending the night. They don't expect you until tomorrow morning."

Morgan snapped her gaping mouth closed. "If you think I'm going to spend the night with you, you are absolutely out of your mind."

"Sure you are, Prof." He looked into her eyes, all traces of humor gone from his face. "I have another set of handcuffs in the glove compartment, and my bed has railings that they hook up to nicely." Noting her expression, he laughed. "Morgan, I'm teasing you. Granted, I'm not above kidnapping a dinner date, but I do stop somewhere short of forcibly dragging my dates to bed."

"Glad to hear it," Morgan rallied. Sometimes she definitely had the feeling that she was over her head with this man. "Are you really going to leave me chained up to your car?"

"Yes, ma'am." He pushed a strand of hair that had fallen out of her bun back behind her ear. "I don't want you to run off by yourself at this time of night. Not to worry, though. I won't be long and I'll lock the car up."

"Thanks a ton," she offered dryly. "I'll be just hunky-dory as long as the car doesn't catch on fire."

He didn't bother to answer. Instead he locked all the doors, climbed out of the car and crossed the lot to the restaurant.

When she was sure he could no longer see her, Morgan stopped scowling. She wasn't really angry with him. The whole thing was kind of fun, and she was putting up a fuss only for the sake of form. He was a crazy man, and she enjoyed him. With a few minor exceptions, like his making her sick the first time she'd met him and his giving her the cold shoulder for a week, she'd found his sense of humor a relief from the sometimes oppressive professionalism of the university.

Her arrest, she was willing to admit, had been kind of funny in an offbeat way, but she did have serious doubts about spending the evening with him. Granted she'd planned to date him once upon a time, but then he had pulled that personality change on her. His rejection had hurt rather badly, even though she hadn't known him long enough to be emotionally involved.

In a way she envied the young women in her class who made a game out of this man-woman thing. She might have been that casual about sex, too, if her life hadn't become so complicated. Simon had been her first real boyfriend. Older, educated, polished, he'd swept her off her feet. By the time she'd touched ground long enough to see that there might be a difference between love and adolescent lust, she was pregnant with Matt.

Simon had been thrilled. He'd been trying to talk her into marriage, but she had resisted. Being head over heels in love at nineteen seemed right to her, but even then she'd known that there was something wrong with being married at nineteen. However, with the doctor telling her that she was going to be a mother in six months, everything had changed, and even her parents had reluctantly agreed to the marriage.

Matt was born four months before her twentieth birthday. Overwhelmed by the physical and emotional demands of parenthood, she had become incredibly dependent on Simon. All her friends were in college, busy with their lives and loves, while her life had revolved around night feedings and bouts of depression.

Simon had enjoyed her dependency and had done one heck of a job making sure she stayed that way. He'd assured her that he would take the responsibility for birth control. Her body had gone through too much for her to be bothered with that, he'd kindly told her. Eleven months after Matt's birth, Steven was added to their family.

Although she hadn't known it at the time, that pregnancy had signaled the marriage's death knell. With the help of her mother, she'd started college soon after Steven's birth. Neither she nor her mother had ever discussed it, but Morgan was sure that both of them knew that her marriage was a mistake and that she'd better be prepared to take care of herself, emotionally and financially.

Amanda was Simon's last-ditch attempt to keep her a subservient, dependent little girl. Morgan could still hardly believe he'd done it, but in the middle of a drag-out battle, he'd admitted to hating her newfound independence and had bragged about sabotaging her diaphragm. This from a man who had a doctorate in philosophy who could, and frequently did, talk for hours about human rights.

When Amanda was born she had shopped around for a doctor willing to tie the tubes of a twenty-two-year-old woman. From then on, she had taken control of her life.

Technically the marriage had lasted three more lousy, cold, embattled years. She struggled to educate herself and grow as a person. Simon had done all he could to block her. The breaking point had come when she'd unexpectedly dropped by his office to have some papers signed and had disturbed him in the act of giving some very private instruction to one of his female graduate students.

In many ways, she was proud of what she'd done with her life. With a tremendous amount of help from her family, especially her mother, she'd educated herself, grown from a child to a rather strong-willed, independent woman and raised three fine children. What she hadn't done however, was come to terms with men, and at this moment, that particular shortcoming had her feeling terribly vulnerable.

Trace jarred her out of her mental meanderings when he opened the car door and set a large bag down beside her.

"If you don't like it, you have only yourself to blame," he growled belligerently.

"I love Chinese food," she answered, looking curiously at his guarded expression.

"Morgan, do you want me to take you home?" He sat beside her, staring straight ahead, refusing to look at her.

"No, not particularly. Why? Do you want to drop me off? It's all right if you do." She tried to sound casual, but her stomach was twisting and her eyes stung. Was he doing it again? Spending only enough time with her to make her feel like a woman, instead of a mother or a teacher, and then dumping her.

Sensing rather than seeing him turn to look at her, Morgan raised her head and looked out the windshield the way he had been doing. The last thing she wanted him to see was her distress. She was a big girl now and could very well hide her emotions until she was alone in her bedroom.

"Why should I want to drop you off? I'm the one who kidnapped you in the first place, remember?" Putting his cool hand against her cheek, he turned her head until she faced him. "Morgan, what's the matter? Are you really upset about this? I kind of thought you'd think it was fun."

"I'm not upset, and it is kind of fun, but—" she hesitated, catching her lower lip pensively in her teeth.

"But?" he prompted her.

"Why were you so mad at me this week and last?"

"Oh, that." Trace started to unfasten the handcuff that was attached to the steering wheel.

"Yes, that," Morgan echoed expectantly.

"Just a little misunderstanding—nothing to worry about." He looked very self-conscious as he made a big production of taking the other cuff off and rubbing her wrist as if the thing had been cutting off her circulation, which both of them knew wasn't true. "Well, let's go eat. I'm starved. Kidnapping professors is hard work."

"Trace."

"You don't really want to get into it now." He looked hopefully at her, but studying her face, he slumped down in his seat in defeat. "I saw your brother coming out of your house the morning after he'd spent the night. I never figured you for a giant blond brother, so I assumed you'd lied. Guess I kind of overreacted," he finished lamely.

"Guess you did," Morgan agreed readily. "Did you feel really stupid when C.J. picked his kids up?" she asked, feeling a weight lift from her shoulders.

"Yes." He shot her a self-deprecating look.

"Good—you deserved to." She smiled at him happily. "As a reward for your honesty, I won't ask you how you happened to see C.J. leaving my house," she offered magnanimously.

Giving her a lopsided, grudging smile, he tilted his head in a gesture of thanks. "I suppose that's more than I deserve."

"Yes, I think it's rather generous of me, too," she teased.

"I knew I should have had you arrested when I had the chance," he growled at her as he started the engine.

LICKING HER FINGERS, Morgan leaned back in the old overstuffed living room chair she'd commandeered when they'd entered Trace's apartment. It had been a choice of the chair, an uncomfortable, student-apartment-style sofa or one of two folding chairs. His home was far different than she'd expected. Not that she'd put much thought into what his home would be like, but this was still a surprise. The place had an unlived-in look to it. No, not really unlived-in, she corrected herself—it was a lived-in mess, but an unloved mess. He only parked his belongings here, and even they didn't look as if they had more than a utilitarian meaning to him. "I like your apartment."

"You do?" He looked around perplexed. "Why?"

"I used to feel bad when you came over to my house. You might have noticed that I'm not very committed to housework. I thought I'd wait until the kids stopped walking all over the furniture before I invested heavily in anything that wasn't Salvation Army quality." A pained look crossed her face when she thought about Matt's preferred way of hanging upside down on the couch to watch TV. "I had visions of you living in some swank bachelor pad, with maid service and piped-in music. Now that I know your bathroom has been condemned by the board of health, I don't feel so bad about mine."

"You have a classy house, Morgan," he told her seriously.

Her twenty-year-old ranch-style tract home might be called a lot of things, but somehow "classy" didn't show up on any of the lists she'd made. Her lists had things like a roof that needed replacing and carpenter ants.

"I mean it, skeptic. It has a good feel to it. A house that people live in. You're not trying to impress anyone with it."

"Good thing," Morgan remarked.

"And even though the atmosphere seems a bit hectic, there's a lot of respect and warmth there."

"Yes, I suppose that if I was pushed, I'd have to agree with you. It seems especially nice when you're not in it with all those warm, hectic children." She wriggled down in the lumpy, comfortable chair, relaxing.

Looking at her as if she had just uttered some earth-shattering news, he whispered, "You're right. We're alone for the first time since I mugged you in the hall. Morgan, why are you wasting so much time?" Lunging playfully at her, he scooped her up and carried her into the bedroom.

"Trace, wait," she cried, choking on her laughter. "You said you didn't kidnap people into bed."

"So I lied," he confessed easily as he lowered her onto the bed. Lying beside her, he looked up at the ceiling. With his elbow he nudged her ribs. "Hey, Teach, wanna neck?"

"I'm not sure," she answered honestly.

"Well, tell me what you're thinking?" He rolled over onto his side and flung an arm across her.

"I don't think this is going to sound very logical, but I'm not sure that, with my kids and all, I should get involved with someone." Grappling with her discomfort, as well as her thoughts, she went on, "And I don't think I'm going to be very good at this kind of thing. I mean, I don't know the rules for affairs, and I'm kind of afraid that you, well, that you're going to be disappointed." All her words seemed to run together.

"All right—let's take this one issue at a time, detective style." He raised up a bit and, supporting himself with his elbow, he started gently tugging the hairpins out of her hair. "This has got nothing to do with your children. They're big kids and they can handle sharing you a bit. If they do get a little bent out of shape, I can handle that and so can you." Running his fingers through her hair, which he'd freed, he smiled gently at her. "I don't know the rules for having affairs with pillars of the community, either, so we'll just have to blunder along and make up our own. We didn't do too badly with your boss this morning, did we? Of course, I could have been more impressive if you had restrained yourself from trying to seduce me, but I guess a guy can't have everything."

"I wasn't seducing you. I was picking on you when you were acting so ferocious. You would be more accurate to think in terms of torture rather than seduction," Morgan corrected him.

"Yes, it was torture," he rumbled meaningfully, "which brings us to your last point." He started kissing her lightly on her mouth, working his way down to her jaw. "I don't think I'm going to be disappointed in our lovemaking, but if things don't turn out so great, we won't hand out reviews. There's a lot more going on between us than sex." Reaching the long column of her throat in his sensuous journey, he found her pulse point and nipped delicately, immediately using his tongue to soothe her. The combination sent shivers down her spine.

Morgan closed her eyes as a heated rush of body-tingling sensation covered her. Dimly she heard him softly clear his throat as if he were forcing himself back to the issue.

"I, for one, will be willing to work on it. And if we don't get it perfect the first time, we'll just practice a lot," he offered nobly. "Morgan, I don't want to pressure you into anything, though my chances of surviving the night are very slim if you leave," he teased. "But will you share my bed with me?"

"Are the sheets clean?" she asked, forcing her eyes open.

"Yes," he lied.

"All right. I guess I can use the money," she commented to no one in particular, as she wound her arms around his neck and tried to pull him down to her.

"What money?" he inquired, holding himself aloft.

"The hundred dollars that goes to the first one in class to bed you," she told him cheerfully, flashing a smile at his stunned look.

"Are you kidding?"

"No."

"How about that—a hundred bucks for my body. Maybe those little girls are brighter than I was giving them credit for." He smirked, pleased with himself.

"Don't get fatheaded. They spend more than that on a pair of boots." Morgan tried to bring him down to earth.

"Huh," he grunted at her. "You're just jealous because I got you here with only a twenty-dollar take-out dinner."

"Of all the nerve." Morgan tried to wriggle free of him, having difficulty maintaining her indignant air.

Laughing, he held her in place. "There's no escape for you. Not now that I know there's money to be made at this." Pinning both of her hands above her head, he lowered his mouth to hers once more, no longer playing.

Using the tip of his tongue, he outlined her lips, familiarizing himself with them before he gently fitted their lips together with a sensual completeness. Moving against her, he sought admission into the damp cavern of her mouth. Willingly Morgan relaxed and invited him to take her wherever he wanted.

She pulled her hands free from his loose grasp and wrapped them around his shoulders. With her fingertips, she explored the world of textures of his broad shoulders, arms and back. He was so solid and warm under her hands. The power and strength of the man was transmitted to her as she stroked the muscles in his arms and back. He brought her alive as nothing else ever had. Everything about him seemed to scream *male* to her long-ignored senses.

Even his scent helped take her to a sensual world where she'd never been before. Simon had smelled of cologne and pipe tobacco. It had been a contrived odor, its purpose similar to that of the huge tomes he lined his office with in order to create his image. Trace, on the other hand, was all clean male animal, and the smell of him made her very hungry for his taste. There was nothing fake about this man, and his masculinity excited her.

His tongue probed and explored her deeply, and Morgan, using her own tongue, joined him in a game of sensual exploration. As the hot, earthy reality of him surrounded her, her world was filled with his essential maleness, closing everything else out. She slipped deeper and deeper into a dark, warm, sensual void. Arching her body up, she mindlessly sought to increase contact. Instinctively she wanted to know the warmth, the feel and the weight of him completely. Holding on to him tightly, she felt an almost frantic need for something she couldn't begin to describe.

"Shh," he whispered in her ear. "Shh. Slow down a little bit, love. We have all night and I want to take it real slow." He kissed her ear, nipping the lobe.

Morgan slowly floated back down to earth with an embarrassed thump. Silently she groaned. She'd blown it. Wanting to go home and cry, she bit her lower lip and lay passively under him.

"Morgan?" He pulled his head back and looked at her.

She closed her eyes, swallowed the lump in her throat and bit her lip a little harder.

"Oh, damn," Trace muttered under his breath. "Morgan, don't look like that. I'm not complaining, I only want this to be good for you. It's all right, love," he pleaded, sprinkling little kisses on her eyes. "Don't freeze up on me now." His hand stroked the side of her body, fitting his palm to the curve of her breast and moving down to her hip. "Are you okay?"

Afraid of what she might betray, she kept her eyes closed and nodded.

"You're such a lousy liar. But tell you what, you just lie there pretending that I can't tell you're upset and I'll kiss it and make it better." Using his lips, he pulled her lower lip out from between her teeth and gently nibbled it seductively.

He nipped and kissed his way down her neck to the V of her blouse. His fingertips brushed across her breast in a delicate circular pattern as he unbuttoned her blouse. One button at a time, he exposed more of her gentle curves to the warmth of his caress.

The heat of passion started building in her once again, only this time she fought it. She'd known that she was going to be terrible for him. She just didn't know enough about men to please him, but she did know that she was going to have to keep control of herself. If she didn't get carried away again, she might figure out what he wanted. It didn't matter any longer whether it was good for her. If she managed to satisfy him, she'd just fake it. At least that was one thing her marriage had given her some skills at. She almost cried from the irony—good old cold Morgan was suddenly too hot.

He unhooked her bra and slipped it off. The feel of his fingertips circling her nipples, lightly running across those sensitive swollen peaks, made her want to cry out in some confused combination of rage, frustration and need. Her back teeth clamped together, and she fought the waves of need that tightened her breasts into aching, throbbing globes.

"Morgan—" the deep voice vibrated against her cheek "—open your eyes."

Licking her lips nervously, she complied with his command. He was leaning over her, watching her with an intent seriousness that seemed at odds with the hand that still moved playfully across one acutely sensitive breast.

"What are you afraid of?" he asked with gentle understanding.

Unable to stop her lips from trembling, she whispered honestly, "I don't want to do anything else wrong." It was all too much for her, and to her mortification she felt tears fill her eyes and start running down the side of her face.

"Oh, love, you're so damned vulnerable," he groaned softly. "You didn't do anything wrong. This isn't a test—

there isn't any right or wrong. We're only trying to find each other's rhythm." He kissed the salty tears from her face. "Stop thinking about it. Let your body take over and don't you do anything but enjoy."

"What if I do something wrong again?" she asked him, embarrassed and unsure.

"You won't do anything wrong. You didn't do anything wrong before. I wish I'd kept my mouth shut," he grated harshly, angry with himself. "I had no idea you were all that unfamiliar with this." His hand stopped its teasing play with her nipple and closed warmly, possessively, over the breast as if both claiming and protecting her at the same time.

"Maybe we should call it quits. Why don't you take me back to my car?" she managed to say with her voice quavering slightly.

"No, Morgan. I'm not letting you go home," he told her with gentle authority. Holding her tightly, he rolled onto his back and pulled her over until she lay on top of him.

Her head pillowed on his shoulder and her breasts flattened against his chest, she relaxed slowly as his hands rubbed her back in a calming pattern.

"Things are just too tense right now. Relax, and everything will work out in time," he said, caressing her.

His gentle touch and understanding words tricked her into lowering her defenses too quickly, and to her surprise and chagrin, she burst into loud racking sobs. Mortified, she tried to escape his hold, but he tightened his arms, keeping her next to him.

"That's right—cry. Let it all out," he encouraged her, rocking her back and forth as if she were a little child in need of his comfort and support.

Giving in, Morgan no longer fought the sobs that poured through her body with loud shuddering tremors. With an abandon generally permitted only to small children, Morgan cried herself into an exhausted sleep.

IT WAS DARK when she woke up, and she needed a moment to remember where she was, but after that everything came back in an awful rush. Talk about blowing it. Her first time in bed with a man in years and she'd cried herself to sleep. And this fine display of mature, feminine sexuality was not for the benefit of just any man. No, it was for the only man that she had been strongly attracted to since adolescence. In the dim light of the bedroom, she looked at the face of the man who lay breathing quietly beside her. She felt like screaming in frustration. She also felt like hiding her head in the sand.

If her car had been here she would seriously have considered slipping out and calling in sick for the rest of the semester. Sighing to herself in self-pity laced with a bit of disgust, she decided to do the next best thing—get herself a glass of water and go back to sleep. The Chinese dinner had made her thirsty, and morning would show up disgustingly early without her staying up half the night thinking about what a fine mess she'd made of things.

Carefully moving away from Trace, Morgan made the significant discovery that she was naked. Smiling ruefully, she slipped out of bed and felt the icy night air on her exposed skin. She had to admit that when she fell asleep she didn't go in for half measures. She slept so soundly that she didn't even wake up when the man she was with got her ready for bed. She had probably been snoring.

Thinking about Trace, she shivered from the cold and quickly felt around in the kitchen cupboard for a glass. She didn't want to face him in the morning. He'd made a joke last night about not surviving without her, but there was no doubt that she'd left him very frustrated when she'd burst into tears. Knowing how miserable Simon had made things when he wasn't gratified, she wasn't looking forward to dealing with Trace. Maybe he would make a couple of cracks and let it go at that. If he got nasty, she wasn't sure how, or if, she could handle it.

Running some water into the glass she found, she considered some other possibilities. He hadn't gotten mad at her last night. Maybe he would just ignore the whole thing, get her home quickly and never call her again. Not a wonderful idea, but a reasonable one. He might say they had a lot going for them besides sex, but sex had to be the biggest part of it, at least for him. After all, there were those 683 relationships that prevented this from being the happily-ever-after kind of thing.

"Why are you stumbling around in the dark?" Trace asked, turning on the kitchen light.

Startled, Morgan spilled the water she was drinking down her naked chest. Jumping back from the sink, she looked around for a towel. "Trace, go away," she begged.

"Turn around," the deep voice said from directly behind her. When she refused to comply, she heard him take an exasperated breath before he gripped her shoulder and turned her. With a towel in one hand, he kept the other hand on her shoulder while he dried her chin and chest.

Eyeing his handiwork, he tossed the towel on the counter. "You certainly are one beautiful lady," he commented in an offhand way, taking his free hand and molding it possessively around one of her breasts. "Umm," he sighed contentedly, wrapping his arms around her and pulling her against his warm, naked body. "I missed you in bed," he whispered in her ear.

"I got up to get a drink," Morgan answered shyly.

"Next time wake me up and I'll get it for you," he ordered, lowering his head until his breath warmed her neck, and she felt his lips seeking out her pulse.

"Okay," she agreed weakly.

"I'm not exactly cold, but let's get back under the covers," he suggested, moving her until she was tucked under his arm.

She got settled on the side of the bed she'd awakened on, then Trace caught hold of her and pulled her back to lie beside him. With his large hands, he gently stroked her body, exploring her curves as if he were committing them to memory. His touch was definitely seductive, and Morgan felt a warm flush cover her skin. His warm caresses seemed more the sure possession of an old familiar lover than merely a lustful exploration.

Under his bold, comfortable touch, she felt herself relax.

"You feel so good," he growled deep in his throat. "So warm and soft. Oh, Morgan, Morgan, Morgan."

Shifting the covers, he lowered his head to her breast, and taking a hardening nipple into his mouth, he began to tease her into taut, throbbing sensitivity.

Morgan let her head roll back as she felt the pulsating pressure start to grow. Clasping his head between her hands, she ran her hands through his hair, experiencing the incredible excitement of having this man make love to her. The little whimpering sounds that she barely heard seemed to be coming from her.

Using his knees aggressively, Trace forced her legs apart. After a fleeting instant of unconscious resistance to being made vulnerable, Morgan relaxed and accepted him as he settled his perspiration-slick body down. The low moan that came from him pushed her body's thermostat even higher until she felt on fire. He wanted her. He wanted her badly, and she knew with certainty that this time she was not going to mess things up.

Pushing his hand between their bodies, he found the source of those ever-tightening tendrils of desire that wrapped themselves around her. As his exploring fingers invaded the damp warmth of her femininity, her world tilted and she arched herself uncontrollably toward the teasing, arousing fingers. He was doing incredible things to her. The whimpering noises coming from her had become a quiet cry.

Responding to her need, Trace raised his head from her breast and slipped his body up the length of hers until she felt pressure of his aroused, powerfully demanding manhood against that sensitized softness. Moving against her in a teasing, testing, tantalizing rhythm, he drove her until Morgan, raising her legs and wrapping them around his hips, pushed against him in an almost desperate attempt to make him complete the union her body screamed for.

With a low cry of satisfaction, Trace thrust deeply into her. Buried in her warmth, he held himself rigid until he felt her body soften and mold itself to his invasion. A sense of rightness enveloped him. Moving slowly against her, he started building the primal forces that would take them to heights that he sensed neither of them had been before.

At his final possession, Morgan surrendered completely to the glowing forces that spun her higher and higher. Playing against the rhythm he established with a hungry female rhythm of her own, she followed him, until with a shudder of almost terrifying passion, she exploded into a thousand bright shiny pieces of glitter. She was so emerged in her own sensations that she barely heard his deep cry as he followed her into oblivion.

Relaxed, Morgan relished the weight of the damp, heavy male as she stroked his back, familiarizing herself with the shape and feel of him. Try as she might, there seemed no way she could control her silly grin.

She'd never felt anything like that before, but she knew that it had been all right. In fact, it had been fabulous. Fabulous for both of them.

As a late starter, she would have a lot to learn, but it might be possible, after all. The kids were, of course, her first priority. They had to be. Then there was her profession that placed as many demands on her as she would permit it. And her family with parents, brothers, brothers' families and so on. Sometimes the list seemed endless with never a spare moment for herself. When she fell into bed at night she counted things left undone rather than sheep. That was the way things went for women who, for one reason or another, ended up doing it all. But now maybe, just maybe, she could have a little magic for herself.

It wouldn't last long—she didn't kid herself on that count. Trace seemed to like her kids and the commotion of her life, but she was sure it was the novelty that appealed to him. Once he got a taste of the responsibilities involved, it wouldn't take long before the complex maze of an active, demanding family would lose its appeal.

But before that time, she'd do all she could to fill a little box in her heart that she'd label Morgan's Great Love. Then, on cold lonely nights, she'd open it and let it warm her.

She'd steal nights like this one, away from the reality of life. She'd invite him to her home for nice family dinners and evenings by the fire, but she'd keep the kids' problems away from him. Let him think they were like some television family with nice, neat concerns that solved themselves humorously in half hour segments.

That would take care of the other little problem she'd foreseen, too. Her children were very attracted to Trace. His male assuredness, strength and calm had a startling effect on her family. The boys and Amanda were fascinated and couldn't seem to get enough of him. It wasn't as if there were no adult males in her house. C.J. had practically lived there since his marriage had started falling apart, and her father had always made a noble effort to do all the things fathers were supposed to do with their children, like fishing trips, camping and father-and-daughter nights. Her children had male models, but none with the appeal of this particular man, who seemed to have fallen asleep on top of her. If the kids became too dependent on Trace they would be hurt badly when he left.

Since she'd never really had a boyfriend, they had not learned how to adapt to the transient nature of a dating relationship. She couldn't allow Trace to become deeply involved with the children's lives. Not that that would be a problem. Men were not known to be particularly eager to adopt some other man's problems.

6

"UP AND AT 'EM," Trace whispered in the ear of the delicate woman who lay curled up so nicely against him.

"Morgan, I see your lips twitching. What you're dealing with here is a highly trained detective with astounding powers of observation. I know a fake when I see one." He brushed her sleek dark hair away from her face. "At least open one eye so I know you're alive and I'll go see about breakfast."

She looked so peaceful lying in his bed that he hated to wake her, but he felt the need to talk with her before he left for work. After last night, he was not willing to take anything for granted. She seemed to have so little self-confidence about sexual matters. He wasn't taking any more chances.

She opened her eyes and looked at him.

"Good morning," he greeted her, hiding the flash of concern when he saw the wary, vulnerable look in her eyes. She looked as if she were waiting to be kicked.

"Good morning. Do you have a robe or something? I think I'd like to take a shower," she said, sounding a bit like a certain professor he knew.

"Good idea. I'll take one with you." He grinned reassuringly. Using his weight subtly to pin her down, he kissed her gently on the lips. She was running scared.

He'd been right to wake her up, even if it was early. Who knew how she'd have reacted to a note?

"Don't be silly," she grumbled, avoiding his eyes.

"Morgan, are you going to tell me what's wrong? Why are you upset? Is it because we slept together?"

After a moment's hesitation, the pensive-looking woman answered. "Okay, I guess a shower sounds like a good idea."

"Sure, and even if it's not a great idea, at least it's the best of two evils, huh?" he teased. Tossing off the covers, he pulled her along with him to the bathroom.

She was approaching what should have been a lovers' playful morning after with all the lighthearted joy one would normally reserve for an execution. She hadn't looked particularly embarrassed to be in his bed, but she was a little apprehensive, and that was beginning to irritate him. They had shared something special last night. She should be trusting him by now, not looking at him as if he were one of the bad guys.

When he had asked her out for dinner, she'd turned him down point-blank. There had been no teasing or subtle come-ons. She'd said no and meant no, period. He'd not been able to let it go at that. Instead, he'd dragged her off to his apartment with every intention of taking her to bed. When she'd made it abundantly clear that she was not an old hand at bedroom recreation activities, he still hadn't backed off. He'd given her enough time to calm down and then he'd seduced her the first chance he'd gotten.

It didn't make sense. He always made sure that the few women he let in his life knew the score. He didn't want anyone getting hurt unnecessarily. He'd always wanted short-term relationships. The no-strings-attached type. So why was he bent on possessing this woman who was commitment, home and family right down to her little toes? Darned if he knew. But he did know he needed to find out what was bothering her and set it straight. He'd deal with the ins and outs of his motivations later, he assured himself.

Over a breakfast of sugar-frosted flakes, she'd come around enough to harass him about the nutritional value of his diet and threaten to subtract points from some diet history. A diet history that he sincerely hoped she had yet to assign the class, because he hadn't the faintest idea what she was talking about.

Deciding he had loosened her up enough, and knowing that he had to leave in twenty minutes, he pounced. "Okay, Prof, I'll have something healthier here for breakfast next time if you tell me what was bothering you this morning."

"I'm not a morning person," she answered quickly, refusing to meet his eyes.

"Sure," he agreed amiably. Walking over to her side of the table, he picked her up, and ignoring her protests, he carried her over to the couch and sat down with her on his lap.

Holding her face between his hands, he kissed her quickly. "This, my pretty lady, is one of the more subtle forms of police interrogation. It may seem like nightsticks and bright lights are more fitting for a criminal, but you'd be surprised how well this works." Kissing her again, he watched her carefully. "For example, right now you're going to be so intimidated that you're going to tell me what was the matter this morning."

"I was just kind of edgy. It's all right now." She lowered her eyes self-consciously and squirmed a little.

"You're going to have to do better than that. I can smell a lie a mile off. In fact, you're such a rotten liar, make that two miles."

Shifting uncomfortably for a few more moments, she evidently gave up. "If you must know, I was uneasy about how you were going to act about last night."

"Act about last night," he repeated thoughtfully. "How did you think I would act?"

"I thought maybe you would be mad or something."

"Morgan, what happened last night was special. How could I possibly be mad?"

"I mean, when I messed things up and then started crying," she whispered.

With a little rush of satisfaction, he knew he'd finally gotten to the truth. She was being honest and vulnerable. His satisfaction, however, was quickly turning into anger. What kind of man had she been married to? He'd seen how she was raising her children. She obviously hadn't grown up in a brutal environment where every exposed weakness was manipulated and used to cause pain. But that was exactly what she expected him to do.

Someone had hurt this lady badly, and he'd bet it was her ex-husband. Making an effort to hide his feelings, he started brushing her face with little kisses. "Morgan, last night was wonderful, all of it. Not just the sex, though that was memorable, too. Last night we shared something with each other. That's special—very special." When she wouldn't respond, he added, "I wouldn't have had last night go any differently than it did, even if I could have planned it to the smallest detail."

Morgan opened her eyes and looked at him unflinchingly. "I told you I wasn't very good at this kind of thing," she said almost hostilely.

"Big deal." He shrugged. "I said we'd practice. I'd love to practice some more right now, but duty calls." He kissed her again. "Get a move on. I have to drop you off at your car."

"Too bad. I guess that's one of the little inconveniences that occur when you abduct your dates," she returned gamely, despite her embarrassment. "And I can't very well move anything with you holding me."

"Complain, complain, complain," he countered, kissing her one last time before heaving himself off the couch and landing her on her feet with the same motion.

THE NEXT NIGHT the intrusive ringing of the phone jarred Morgan out of a deep sleep. Groping on her bedside table for the phone, she glanced at the clock. Two-twenty. If it was for one of the kids heads would roll.

"Hello," she grunted into the mouthpiece.

"Good morning, pretty lady. Did I wake you?" the disgustingly jolly male voice asked her.

"No, you didn't wake me. I'm in the kitchen baking cookies," she answered sarcastically. She hadn't been lying when she'd told Trace that she wasn't a morning person. However, she was even less of a middle-of-the-night person. Since the kids had started sleeping through the night, she'd lost all tolerance for being wakened. "Was there some reason you called, or is this some new form of police harassment?"

"You wound me, madam. This is important police business." Morgan snorted in response to his dramatics.

"I'm making a survey. Do you know where your children are?" he asked her cheerfully.

Waking up a bit, Morgan heard background noise from his call. He was still at work. The man must work horrendous hours. "Why, yes, Officer. Let me see. My daughter's at her father's. My youngest son is asleep in his room, and my oldest son is asleep at a friend's house. Did I pass?"

"As a matter of fact, you didn't do any better on my test than I did on yours," he admonished her playfully.

"What are you talking about, Trace?" She was no longer playing.

"Matt was brought in to me a little while ago," he informed her calmly.

"Matt was brought in to you? Trace, is he all right?" she asked, making a not very successful attempt to control her anxiety. Homicide? Matt brought into homicide?

"He's fine. I didn't mean to frighten you. Everything is all right. Don't worry," he quickly assured her, belatedly realizing how she might interpret things.

Releasing the breath she'd been holding, Morgan said, "Please tell me what happened. And, Trace, I do not consider this to be a time when humor is acceptable."

"Yes, Mother," he replied apologetically, with a great deal more laughter in his voice than suited her. "Matt was brought in to the front desk a while ago for trespassing. He's not really in any trouble. The officer who spotted the boys wanted to get them off the streets."

"Where was he, and what was he doing at this time of night? This isn't making a whole lot of sense to me, Trace."

"That's because you are not a thirteen-year-old male. The way I got the story, he and two friends were playing in some drainage pipes out by Highway 96. A modification of Dungeons and Dragons with a little bit of Conan the Barbarian tossed in to keep it macho. They weren't doing any damage, but the freeway is not the safest place to play, nor is midnight a particularly healthy hour for kids."

"Do you know who he was with?" she asked grimly.

"Yes. Let's see. Here they are." He found the boys' names and read them to her. Hearing her intake of breath, he asked, "What's wrong? Something about these two that's a problem?"

"Yes, one of those boys is the one that I think broke into our house. Matt has been forbidden to play with him. The kid comes from a troubled home, and even though I understand the reasons he's acting out, I don't want Matt involved in his problems. Matt creates enough problems on his own," Morgan explained distractedly. How do you deal with a kid who was bigger than you and had flagrantly disobeyed you? "How did you get involved in all this?"

"When they asked him who to contact he gave them my name. I think he was trying to pull some strings," he added dryly. "I was still here, so I went down and took care of things."

"Should I come down and pick him up? They're not going to put him in jail or anything, are they?" Morgan asked.

"Umm, well, not exactly." He suddenly sounded uncomfortable.

"Trace, please tell me what's going on. This is driving me crazy."

"Well, he was a little bit belligerent," Trace started to tell her.

"I bet," Morgan couldn't help commenting.

"Yes. I kind of gathered, by some of the things he said to me, that he was not happy about you being with me last night."

Morgan laid her head down on the pillow and sighed. Matt hadn't said much to her, but what he hadn't said had been worrisome.

"Morgan, Matt is a big kid and he's going to be making decisions on his own. You can't lock him away in his room," he told her argumentatively.

"Trace, I'm not disagreeing with you. Will you please just tell me what you've done and then we can argue about it."

Sounding as if he was braced for a battle, he finally answered her. "I locked him up with a cellmate who was guaranteed to encourage Matt to stay on the safe side of the law, no matter how mad he gets at you."

The silence seemed to last forever. Finally Morgan broke it with a very soft and very dangerous voice. "You locked my child up with a dangerous criminal?"

"No, Morgan. Calm down. I had him locked up with a cop. All he did was talk rough, and not even that rough. Matt doesn't know he was a cop, however, and the kid's a bit shaken up. I wouldn't put him in any danger," he defended himself, obviously a little put out that she had thought differently. "But look, if he's going to go through this kind of rebellion he needs to know what he's playing around with." When she didn't answer him for a few moments, he asked tentatively, "Morgan, are you mad?"

"Yes, but I'm not sure I should be. It's going to take me a little while to reconcile my instinct to protect him with his need to make his own mistakes." After a momentary pause she went on, "I think maybe I should thank you, but would you mind taking a rain check on it? I think now it might make me choke."

"Take as long as you want." He sounded relieved.

"Should I come down and pick him up?" She controlled her voice carefully. This was all a bit much to have to handle right out of a deep sleep. It wasn't the first time Matt had been in trouble with the authorities, but before it had been school personnel and the fire department. Police and jail had such a serious sound.

"No, I'm almost finished up here. I'll drop him off. And, Morgan..."

"Yes," she prompted when he hesitated.

"This is none of my business, but the kid has had a lot to deal with tonight and he needs to think some things through on his own. I don't think you need to add anything to it," he told her reluctantly, as if dreading to make the suggestion, but feeling he had to.

"You mean ignore the whole thing?"

"Yes, I guess that's what I mean."

"I'll think about it," she answered stiffly. "Thank you for calling and for bringing him home."

"Yes, ma'am," he replied, just as scrupulously polite. "I'll see you tomorrow, right?"

"Yes, tomorrow," she replied flatly, before hanging up the phone.

TWO HOURS PASSED before she heard Matt come in. When he headed down the basement stairs, she laid her head back on the pillow. Trace had been right. She didn't need to get involved in this. In fact, she'd spent the past two hours trying to think of a way to handle the situation and had come up with nothing. Matt was angry with her, and his behavior had been designed to get even. Any anger, tears or expression of fear on her part would just increase his wish for revenge.

In the morning she'd see if he wanted to talk about it, and if he was ready to deal with her relationship with Trace, but that would be it. Trace, hopefully, had handled the rest.

Trace, Morgan thought to herself with a sigh. Was it only last night she had vowed to keep him uninvolved with her family's concerns? If she continued to handle this affair with as much grace as she'd shown so far, it would be the shortest affair in the history of womankind. The box she was planning to hide her warm memories in would have to be a matchbox.

LAUNDRY—SHE HATED laundry. The only job more horrible was dishes, Morgan thought as she pulled another load of clothes out of the dryer. Dishes were the worst because a clean sink lasted all of two minutes before someone dumped a glass into it. At least laundry only had to be done a couple of times a week. Writing—now that was a job she loved. Someone calls you up and makes you feel important by asking you to contribute to a book. You strain your brain for twenty or so pages and send it off. Before you know it, there you are, part of a big impressive-looking text, and you only have to do the job once every few years.

Apparently Trace had handled things well enough last night so Matt only had to be dealt with once, too. Sorting through the pile of clean clothes for shirts and dresses to be hung up before they wrinkled, she replayed the events of the morning. Matt had come in and talked with her while she was still in bed. He'd apologized for making her worry about him, and he'd lectured her about how stupid it was for a person to act like a jerk because they had gotten mad about something. Looking very uncomfortable, he'd then asked her how she felt about Trace.

Deciding he deserved honesty, she'd admitted to liking Trace very much. Matt, kicking the side of her bed the entire time, apologized again. He told her that he also kind of liked Trace, but he didn't think the man would be back. Apparently Matt had said a few very nasty things to him last night.

Picking up the full basket, Morgan turned to head upstairs. When she pushed the laundry room door open, she ran head-on into the very man she'd been thinking about.

"Trace, you startled me. Did one of the kids tell you I was down here?"

"No. No one answered the door, so I walked in and wandered around until I found you. Just as anyone else could have done," he informed her pointedly.

"Oh—guess I didn't have the door locked again, huh?" she answered sheepishly, as the large man took the basket out of her hands.

"Guess so. Do you ever have it locked?" He shot the question at her as she preceded him up the stairs.

"Usually when we leave, we lock it," she mumbled under her breath.

"Good thinking, Morgan. Keep your junk safe, while leaving yourself wide open."

"Did you come here just to yell at me?" So she didn't lock her door—this was a nice neighborhood and nothing terrible had ever happened in it. The worst she had heard about had been her own burglary. And just how did you keep a door locked when you had three kids who each had twelve million friends in and out all day long? Hire a butler?

"No, I guess not," he admitted almost reluctantly. "I came to fix the dead bolt, kiss you hello and maybe take you all out to dinner."

"Dump the laundry out here." She motioned to her bed. When his hands were empty, she moved in closer and slid her arms up around his neck. "Do you have to do it in that particular order?" Smiling, she wove her fingers through the thick dark blond hair, urging him to bend his head.

"No." His lips twitched in a half smile as he ran his hands down her back until they firmly cupped the full curves of her derriere. He pulled her into the warm cradle of his hips. With one hand on the back of her head, he held her as his lips descended to take hers.

She'd missed this man, she realized as she let the taste and feel of him sink her into a state of sensual semiconsciousness. She'd been afraid to admit it before, for fear that Matt had managed to drive him away, but now that he was back, she was free to let her longing for him show in her hands that roved hungrily over his well-muscled shoulders and back.

"Are the kids home?" he whispered on a harshly drawn breath.

"Yes," she moaned in return.

"Wonderful," he groaned.

Still stroking him, she moved away from his warmth. She could feel the enticing imprint of his solidness against her soft, giving flesh, but this was not the time to indulge such sensations. "Have you had lunch yet?"

"What do you have in mind?" he rumbled seductively, trying to pull her back into his embrace.

"Down, boy. I was thinking in terms of a tuna sandwich."

"If that's the best I can get, then I guess I'll settle for it," he replied morosely, giving her a quick kiss on her nose.

Morgan had just set a plate of sandwiches on the table for Trace and the boys when Amanda came flying in the front door, back from a visit with her father and stepmother. "Hi, everyone, I'm home!" she shouted. "Look at my new sweater. Annette helped me pick it out. Isn't it great?" The ten-year-old danced into the kitchen, modeling her new finery. "Trace, what are you doing here?" she squealed delightedly.

"Eating lunch. I like your sweater, Amanda," he complimented the beaming child.

"Yes," she agreed without any hint of modesty. "Annette's taste is loads better than Mom's. That's why Daddy married her when he got tired of Mom." Flashing her mother a scornful look, she turned to Trace once again. "I'm so glad you're here. I didn't think you would be. After all, Mom chases all her boyfriends away, one way or another."

"Amanda, that's enough. If you would like lunch and think you can remember your manners, please wash up," Morgan told her sternly. Fat lot of good being stern would do when Amanda was in this mood. After spending the day with her father and stepmother, Amanda was always full of criticism for everyone, particularly for her mother. Steven, who had once gone for an afternoon with Amanda, reported that Annette found multiple opportunities to make snide comments about Morgan. Amanda defended her mother tooth and nail, but after standing up for her mother for a day, Amanda somehow felt the need to repeatedly insult Morgan. One of the many joys of visitation rights.

"It's true. You chased Bob away just when he was starting to be some fun." She tossed her chestnut hair back in a gesture that didn't belong on a ten-year-old child.

"Amanda." The definite threat in Morgan's voice seemed to reach the pugnacious girl. Shooting her mother another nasty look over her shoulder, she flounced off.

"She's such a creep," Matt complained. "Why don't you just let her go live with them? After a week or so, she wouldn't think Frankenstein's Daughter was all that wonderful."

"Sisters are one of life's trials and tribulations," Morgan informed him good-naturedly.

Amid the usual noise and commotion, they forgot about Amanda, who had apparently decided to pout in her room rather than eat, and settled down to enjoy lunch. Trace was again the center of attention, this time answering the questions Matt had about police work. One night in the slammer, and he was ready to rework the entire operation. Relieved that Trace and Matt seemed to have no hard feelings toward each other, Morgan relaxed and listened to Trace consider Matt's suggestions. Much to Matt's delight, Trace even found merit with some of the teen's ideas.

It wasn't until Morgan started the dishes that she had any hint that all was not well.

Leaning his large frame against the counter, Trace flicked a dish towel in her general direction. "So, Professor, what did you do with the body?"

"What body?"

"Bob's."

"I don't know what you're talking about." Morgan started washing the dishes, handing him the rinsed ones to dry.

"Morgan, confess. I've seen convicted murderers look less guilty than the three of you when good old Bob was brought up." He swatted her lightly on the rump with the dish towel. "Out with it, lady, before I get rough."

"Are you sure the boys looked guilty?" she asked him, bothered a little by his suggestion. She knew, of course, exactly how she and her sons had been reacting. When he nodded she winced.

"Out with it, Morgan."

Shooting him an indignant look, she complied. "Let me ask you some questions first, okay?"

"Shoot."

"If Steven and Matt wanted to wrestle with you, would you agree to it?" She dried her hands with the towel Trace held and leaned back against the counter opposite him so she could watch him.

"Steven? Yes, probably. Matt? No, I don't think so. He'd make me humiliate him in order to restrain him. He's a good kid, Morgan, but a little too hostile and competitive for that kind of play." He shrugged his shoulders in helpless apology.

"How about Amanda? Would you wrestle with her?"

"No," he answered emphatically.

"Why not?"

"Morgan, she's just a little girl, not even close to a woman yet, but she's playing little flirty female games. It's fine with me if she wants to polish her act around me, but I don't think I want to encourage that or frighten her with physical-contact games." He looked uncomfortable. "Why are you asking me this? Is it some kind of test?"

"If it was, you passed with flying colors," she assured him. "Bob was a guy I dated only a couple of times. Unlike you, he did wrestle with the kids. With Matt it was a disaster, and with Amanda it just kind of made me uncomfortable." Seeing a downright aggressive look appear in his eyes, she hastened to reassure him. "It wasn't anything to get upset about. They just horsed around, and I was there all the time. I just didn't like it. A gut feeling that probably meant nothing, but it made me lose all interest in Bob. For one reason or another, I had trouble getting rid of him."

"Finish it, Morgan," he ordered when she hesitated a moment.

"Well, it so happened that Bob has a real phobia about snakes," she told him.

"Now it's starting to make sense. Hence the posters on the basement door of poor barbarian female slaves with snakes wrapped all around their bodies?" he asked with a grin.

"Did you by any chance notice the one of the huge boa with the half-swallowed barbarian that's on Amanda's door? That's Matt's idea of interior decorating." She returned his smile. "After Bob had been hanging around awhile, Matt became very interested in snakes. So interested that he borrowed money from Steven and bought a small anaconda. Unfortunately the thing happened to escape in the living room and we've yet to find it."

Morgan looked pointedly at the floor, waiting for his reaction. When none came, she risked a peek at him. Catching his eye, they both started laughing.

"Was Steven in on it, too?" he asked after a moment.

"I guess. The loan was interest free. That's an almost unheard-of phenomenon around here."

Shaking his head in wonder, the grinning man asked, "Does it make you nervous to have kids brighter than you?"

Morgan stopped smiling. "Yes."

"Morgan?"

"All my kids are bright enough, but you have to multiply my IQ to get Matt's," she told him grimly, staring at the dirty dishes but not seeing them.

"Are you sure?"

"Very. He's a tested and certified genius." After a minute she went on. "He's starting math classes at the university this January."

"Poor Morgan," he commiserated, walking over and wrapping his arms around her. He held her tightly, letting her lean on him for a little while.

Morgan accepted his warmth and comfort. Most people thought it was wonderful to have a kid with Matt's intelligence, but this man seemed to understand how difficult it made things. Teachers never knew what to do with him, boring classes turned him into a horrible discipline problem, and she was never really sure she was handling things right, either. When IQs were as high as Matt's, even the experts couldn't give her hints on understanding how his mind worked.

"Enough standing around the kitchen. Time to get back to work." He slapped her rump playfully.

"What's with you? Have you been reading Matt's barbarian books?" she accused before slipping out of his arms and tackling the dishes.

WATCHING THE MAN sitting across the restaurant table, Morgan smiled ruefully. The day certainly hadn't turned out the way she'd planned, but it had been one of the best Sundays she'd had in a long time.

Trace had kicked around the house, fixing doors, helping Steven set up bookshelves, driving Amanda out to the stables, and even going with Morgan while she shopped for the week's groceries. If she had tried, she couldn't have submerged him any further in her family activities.

"Morgan, I didn't know you were going out to dinner tonight," a male voice said behind her.

With a silent groan, she turned in her seat and confirmed her suspicions. This was one member of her family she really hadn't wanted Trace to come across for quite a while. "Ross, how nice to see you. Are you here with your family?"

When he nodded and continued to size Trace up, Morgan stopped trying to postpone the inevitable. "Trace Standon, this is my brother, Ross Wilson."

"Mr. Standon, nice to meet you. Are you with the university by any chance?" her older brother asked in the pompous way she'd always detested.

"Yes, in a way," Trace answered. His face was bland, but Morgan could see little lights of mischief dancing in his eyes. "I'm a student in one of Morgan's undergraduate classes."

Morgan felt like strangling her brother when he straightened and looked down at Trace. She and C.J. had once snapped a picture of him practicing that look in the bathroom mirror when he was a teenager.

"Aren't you a little old to be taking undergraduate classes?" he asked sarcastically.

"Yes, but it's a special program. I can earn a high school diploma at the same time," Trace told him seriously, refusing to acknowledge Morgan's wide-eyed warning glare.

"Oh, my!" her pompous jerk of a brother exclaimed.

Matt, not able to see that Trace was playing with his uncle, jumped into the conversation. "I don't think he's too old to go back to school. After all, I bet you're older than he is and you haven't left it yet to get a job."

"Son, I work at the university. That is my job," he explained condescendingly to the fuming boy.

"Yes, but it's not a real job. The university will let anyone with the money go to it. If you're too chicken to leave, then they kind of have to make you a teacher, otherwise it's embarrassing for them," Matt fired back.

Before Ross could recover from this unexpected attack, or Morgan could try to call a halt to the squabbling, Amanda entered the fray. "Trace has a real job. He's a detective. That's a lot better than making people read boring stories that Neanderthal men wrote."

"Morgan, can't you control your children?" Her brother looked around at her brood disgustedly.

"No, she can't. You see, Matt's a genius and you have to be very careful otherwise you'll damage the mind that might very well find the cure for cancer or make an amazing discovery about the solar system." Steven looked like a concerned angel as he smiled up at Ross and twisted the knife a little more deeply into his uncle's body. "He's the one that's going to make our family famous. I bet in a few years people will be wanting to interview you so they can write books about Matt."

Morgan debated with herself whether to laugh or slip under the table and hide. Ross was far from her favorite brother, but watching her offspring gang up on him was almost painful. It surprised her that they'd gone into their pack attack for Trace. Matt rarely leaped up to do battle for anyone other than himself and his immediate family. As a general rule, he liked to watch adults have it out, and had even been known to set up confrontations between teachers and counselors just for the heck of it.

This time, however, it wasn't Matt sitting back and enjoying the flying sparks, it was Trace. Much to her annoyance, he leaned back from the table and watched her children defend him with undiluted enjoyment. Morgan tried to kick him under the table. Unfortunately she got Matt instead.

"Ow. Mom, Matt kicked me," Amanda complained loudly.

"You kicked me first," Matt defended himself.

"Honestly, Morgan, perhaps you ought to consider not allowing them out in public until you can improve their manners. It's a shame that their father was not permitted to have a larger role in shaping them." Her dearly beloved English professor brother delivered his parting shot as he strutted away to join his well-mannered one-child family.

Morgan glared at each member of her family, one at a time. One by one they became uncomfortable. That is, they did until she got to Trace. When she turned her basilisk stare on him, the man had the nerve to start shaking, and it wasn't fear causing the tremors. It took only a few seconds before his condition passed to the children, but because they had less self-control, their laughter was not quiet or contained. Looking at the group around her trying to stifle its laughter behind hands or napkins, she gave up and started giggling, too.

7

LEANING BACK in Morgan's chair, Trace glanced at her office clock. Ten minutes and she'd be finishing up her class, which he'd again missed. This time his only excuse was oversleeping. Last night he'd left her house early, but had been up for hours trying to come to some agreement with himself about what he wanted out of this relationship.

He liked the lady. He liked the lady a lot. Her humor and warmth seemed to draw him like magnets. He even liked her kids, he thought with an ironic smile. While he didn't particularly appreciate the strategic problems of arranging for some time alone with Morgan, her kids certainly kept things from getting dull.

Dinner last night had to be one of the more interesting meals he'd eaten. After they'd come so nobly to his defense, the kids' behavior had degenerated into Matt ordering Amanda to assume the "slave position" on her knees. That resulted in a major battle with Amanda threatening in a loud hiss to use his liver as a target for her butter knife. Steven had livened things up a bit, too, when he'd announced that, because of the current rate of inflation, he was going to have to raise the interest rate on all outstanding loans.

Morgan and her family were like a breath of fresh air, but there were some major problems. Looking distastefully at the stacks of papers on her desk, he put his feet on them and tipped back until the chair balanced on two legs. That was one of the problems. Her older brother was a fool, and even though Morgan didn't seem to hold any of the man's beliefs, the fact remained that she was a lot better educated than Trace. He'd lied about not having a high school diploma, but it wasn't much of a lie.

He wouldn't have stayed in school past sixteen if he hadn't had the good fortune to steal a red Corvair for a joyride. It hadn't been the first car he'd taken, but it was the one that had gotten him busted. His arresting officer was of the old school. After bullying him a bit and reducing the smart-mouthed punk to a scared kid, Raymond had driven him home.

He remembered the night vividly. The big burly cop walking him up the stairway, past dripping, stinking bags of garbage, to his mother's door. Raymond knocked repeatedly and, after what seemed an eternity to the slump-shouldered scrawny kid being held up by his collar, his mother had finally answered the door. Drunk, her angular body half covered by a ratty robe, she guarded the door with one hand while holding a bottle with the other. The deep-voiced cop had tried to explain what had happened, but Trace's mother hadn't listened. With a slurred yell, she'd told the entire building that she wanted nothing more to do with the white trash son that cur of a husband had left her with. She'd ended up slamming the door in their faces.

The uniformed man looked at the closed door for a moment and then turned to Trace, shrugging his massive shoulders. "Ain't life a scream" had been his only comment before he'd dragged Trace back down the stairs and out of the tenement.

From that moment on, his life changed drastically. Raymond, for some never-explained reason, had taken the humiliated kid home with him. The old cop's place was not much better than his mother's, but it was clean, and there was always enough food to fill up a perpetually hungry sixteen-year-old. There were a few other things too, like a heavy-handed cop who told Trace to be home by nine, who actually looked at his report cards and, taking one look at his friends, told him to kiss them goodbye.

Raymond was the one who had gotten him into police work. Trace couldn't imagine doing anything different with his life. The only reason he was working on his undergraduate degree in criminal justice was that the department wanted him to have it and they were letting him arrange his hours around classes. He'd enjoyed the experience, and he might consider taking another class now and then, but he had no intention of ever going after another degree or doing anything other than police work.

Which brought up another problem. Being a cop was not necessarily the safest profession, though it wasn't nearly as risky as some people believed. Raymond had died of the same heart condition that nailed executives in big, safe offices. But cops didn't have the greatest track record for staying married. Maybe it was the pressure, or more likely the kind of man that went into police work, but the profession's divorce rate was high. Really high.

That had been the excuse he'd given himself for the uncommitted relationships he'd sought with women. There were other reasons a little closer to home, however—the most important being his own lack of a decent family. You learned how to get along in a family by being raised in one. What he'd learned about family life was nothing he wanted to pass on to any upcoming generation.

He heard the office door open, and he fully expected to see Morgan. When the carefully groomed, dark-haired man with a touch of gray at his temples walked in, Trace had no problem placing him as another professor. The newcomer took one look at Trace's feet on Morgan's desk and his lips curled in a condescending smile, and Trace was willing to bet he was talking to another of Morgan's brothers.

"Do you have a meeting with Dr. Harris?" the professor asked coldly.

"Do you?" Trace countered, with no more warmth in his voice than the professor's.

"I hardly consider that to be any of your business."

Trace's reply was lost when the door opened again and Morgan walked in. Noting Trace at her desk with a flicker of surprise, she turned to her other visitor.

"I don't believe you have any reason to be here," she told the man with an icy intensity that caused Trace to stiffen.

"Don't be ridiculous, Morgan. We have a great deal that needs to be discussed. It only makes sense that we sit down like rational adults and discuss it," the man replied impatiently. "Why don't you ask your, umm—" he hesitated insultingly, as if searching for the right word "—colleague? to leave and we can get down to business."

"I'm not asking him to leave because he's welcome. With you I have nothing to discuss, but if you feel you need to talk with me, do it through my lawyer."

Trace watched her carefully. Her intense reaction to this rather pompous and seemingly ineffectual man was unexpected. His request for something as commonplace as a mere conversation had her fighting as if her back were up against the wall. He was relieved that she hadn't asked him to leave. He wouldn't have left her to face whatever she was dealing with alone, but he appreciated her willingness to assign him the role he had every intention of assuming, anyway.

"Morgan, get rid of him," the attractive-looking man snarled, dropping his polished facade.

"No," she answered emphatically. "He's welcome to hear anything you apparently feel you must say to me."

"How interesting," he drawled sarcastically. "Don't tell me that you are actually condescending to allow a man into your frigid life."

"Morgan, introduce us." Trace stood up and faced the man.

"Detective Standon, this is my ex-husband, Simon Harris," Morgan introduced them in a flat voice.

"So, Detective, as you can see this is a family matter, and I think it would be better if you left." Simon had regained his composure and looked at Trace as if he was seeing something distasteful that had flown in through an open window.

"You and I are very far from being a family, and as I explained earlier, anything you have to say to me can be said through my lawyer." Some of Morgan's iciness had turned into anger.

"You heard the lady—she asked you to leave. If you'd like to be escorted out, I'd look forward to the privilege." Trace moved a step closer.

"Oh, honestly. This is absurd, Morgan. I hardly need to go through a lawyer to discuss an academically advanced school on the East Coast that we should be sending Matt to," he complained as he stepped backward.

"Yes, you do need to go through my lawyer for that, or any other concern."

"Morgan, grow up," he snapped nastily over his shoulder as he turned and slammed out of the office door.

The bang of the door echoed in the suddenly painfully silent room. Pensively smoothing her already sleek hair, Morgan turned to face Trace. "Why weren't you in class?" she challenged.

Trace smiled in reassurance. "I'll make you a deal, Professor. Come here and let me hug you and I won't ask you any questions about what that was all about. Today," he added as an afterthought.

"Deal," she agreed in a wobbly voice as she walked over to him and hid her face against his chest.

Wrapping his arms around her, he held her tightly, rubbing her back. As he kissed the top of her head he realized with a start that he had comforted this woman more times than he had made love to her. And what struck him as even stranger, he was more than willing to give her a whole lot more comfort if she needed it. In fact, he would be very unhappy if she turned to anyone else when she was upset. Shaking his head at his own folly, he promised himself that sometime very soon he would really figure out what was going on.

"OKAY, MARTHA. Now, when you are under the water, blow out all your breath. When we see the bubbles stop, we'll read the scales and motion for you to come up. Do you think you understand, honey?" Morgan asked the skinny teenager who stood in her bathing suit beside the modified hot tub.

When the girl nodded, Morgan rechecked the suspension scale her subject would be sitting on underwater, and motioned for her assistant to start recording numbers.

Part of the current research she was doing on body imagery was on the relationship between perception and the percentage of total body fat. A hundred pounds on one kid could mean thirty percent fat, and on another kid it meant only fourteen percent. It all depended on what kind of physical shape they were in, and it made a tremendous difference in their appearance. The heavier a person weighed suspended in water, the more his or her body was made up of muscle and bone.

The procedure was relatively simple unless one was dealing with very obese people, which meant one had to strap weights to the subjects in order to keep them from floating to the surface. But the trickiest group she'd ever worked with had been a group of lean, trim fire fighters that she'd run through the lab as a public service during a Fitness Awareness Week. Who would have guessed that out of the dozen or so she'd had to test, four would be terrified of water. Getting that group to empty their lungs under three feet of water had turned out to be a real trick.

But even those public servants hadn't caused her the problems that the one public servant that she had not seen in almost a week was causing. After having witnessed the awkward scene between herself and Simon, Trace had hugged her, kissed her and told her he would see her soon. His definition of *soon* seemed to be significantly different from hers.

She might have thought that Trace was running for cover, except that he was calling her almost every night. According to him, things had fallen apart at work and he was spending almost every waking hour trying to put them together again. Paranoid as she was, she'd considered the possibility that he was weaning her off him. But that flight into self-pity was stopped by the newspaper accounts of what was happening in town.

Now that the boys had an "in" at the police station, they pored over the morning newspaper, looking for reports of people dying. They weren't fussy about how the poor souls died. Knifings, robberies, car accidents, even innocent-sounding heart attacks could be, and frequently were, cover-ups for diabolically clever killings. This was just the way life was, the two Sherlock Holmeses, who kept her from overeating at breakfast, assured her. However, even allowing for vivid imaginations, the paper did seem to be reporting a large number of uncommonly violent incidents.

She was a bit surprised and not pleased by the extent to which she missed the man. Not that she was pining away or even in a blue funk—she just found herself wishing he was with her to share something that she knew he'd find funny, with his twisted sense of humor.

Her sleep, too, was suffering from Trace's schedule, or lack of one. He called her whenever he had a few minutes, be it seven at night or four in the morning. She was so pleased to hear from him that she didn't even complain about being wakened, which was ominous.

Their conversations were a bit ominous, too. They weren't at all what she'd imagined lovers' private conversations to be. No flowers, no compliments, no intimate sharing of deep inner feelings. Their conversations were more like interrogations, with Trace asking and Morgan answering. He'd held himself back from asking about Simon, but as far as she could tell, that was his only restriction.

He'd demand a moment-by-moment description of what she'd done all day, and then another accounting of the children's day. What had they said at dinner? Had Matt found the money to pay Steven off and get out from under that twenty-two percent interest? Did Amanda go riding and did she get that leather strap replaced on her hakamore? On and on. Morgan found herself paying closer attention to her children because she knew sometime during the night she'd have to take an oral exam.

Sandwiched between questions about the kids he'd toss in a few to her. How many brothers did she have? How educated was her father? That one she thanked Ross for. Among the normal, getting-to-know-you variety of questions, he'd flatten her with doozers like, "Are you worried about being pregnant?" When she'd answered no, he had gotten indignant and wanted to know why a woman who hadn't slept with someone for years was on birth control pills. According to the expert gynecologist on the other end of her phone, "They aren't even good for someone as old as you are." Not sure whether she was pleased with his show of concern, irritated by his thinly veiled accusation, or too decrepit from her rapidly advancing age to respond, she'd taken a long time to choke out why her getting pregnant was impossible. Then, when she'd had the perfect opening, she'd lost her courage and hadn't asked him how he felt about it. Was it presumptuous to ask someone earmarked Lover Only if he wanted kids of his own? Probably, but she really wished she knew what he thought.

SHE'D DONE IT AGAIN. Why, oh why, did she have to wake up in the middle of the erotic dreams that were starting to plague her? Why couldn't she finish the dream at least once? Maybe she hadn't ruined it—maybe she was still asleep, she thought sleepily. Paying careful attention, she wiggled both her hands. Her hands were definitely not the ones that were gliding sensuously over the fullness of her breast, flicking her nipples gently with the passing of each finger. Her hands were safely weaving themselves through the soft hair on his chest. His chest?

Jerking upright, Morgan rocked unsteadily on the bed. Even though she was confused and half-awake, there was no missing the soft male laughter that came from the dimly outlined, nude man lying on the bed beside her.

"Trace, what are you doing here? Did I forget to lock the door again?" she asked, dazed.

"What do you think I'm doing here? I'm the sandman invading your dreams, of course. And yes, you actually did have the door locked, miracle of miracles. Steven let me in." He reached over and pulled her back down beside him.

"How did Steven hear the door?" she asked, her mind starting to clear. Steven had once slept through the scream of a smoke detector that had gone off in the basement when Matt had roasted marshmallows on a light bulb.

"He was up waiting for me. But now that I'm here he's gone to bed, and I've locked your bedroom door, after placing a skull and crossbones on it to scare away visitors, so will you please be quiet and get on with your dream," he growled provocatively in her ear.

"What makes you think I'm having that kind of dream about you?" she prevaricated, letting her fingers return to the interesting nest they'd discovered in her sleep.

He nuzzled her neck, getting lost in the delicious sensations. "Because, as I shouldn't have to remind you, I'm the detective. And besides, I've been having the same dream on a regular basis."

"Oh, tell me about your dream," she whispered, letting her fingers trace the hard planes of his chest as she searched for his nipples.

"I'm chasing after the mere shadow of a woman who's stomping through the snow, pretending the stuff she's mashing with her boots is my head." He ran his hands along the length of her, molding them to her every curve, while at the same time kissing a teasing pattern down her neck and chest, carefully avoiding her tingling breasts. "As I get closer, I can clearly make out the sweet, full curves of her." By this time his hands had found her breasts and were lovingly cupping them. Slipping one hand erotically into the cleft between the soft mounds, he let his fingers caress her with intimate tenderness.

At his touch Morgan felt a wave of pleasure sweep over her. No longer able to keep her eyes open, she let them close as her head fell back.

"Finally catching her, I turn her around. As she kicks my shins, I rip her blouse off and take a lovely, dusty-rose nipple in my mouth." He kept on with his story, using his tongue to lick her nipples until she was ready to scream. "Then I kiss my way down to the heart-shaped mole right below her belly button." He proceeded to follow his own story line, leaving her breast to start a path of kisses down her midline.

Moaning with frustration when he left her breasts, Morgan came up a little from her sensual fog. "What heart-shaped mole?"

Lifting his head, he surveyed her flat stomach with a great show of surprise. "Hey, how about that, no mole." He kissed her belly, drawing circles with his tongue. "That must have been some other professor. We'll go back to the dusty-rose nipples, I guess," he declared calmly, moving up her body to take a throbbing nipple in his mouth and suck it boldly.

"What other professor?" she spat out.

Morgan leaned on her elbow and glared at the man who was, without question, the most infuriating person she had ever met, and who was also laughing hard enough to start the bed rocking. "Not funny, Officer."

"Yes it is, Professor," he disagreed. "But for some reason you don't look like you're in the mood to appreciate it." Trace, chuckling, grabbed her and pulled her resisting body over his until she lay on top of him. He stroked her hair back from her face with one hand as he kept the other on the small of her back, pinning her to him. "Morgan, you are the only professor I have ever taken to bed. I don't even know anyone with a heart-shaped mole—I was just seeing if you were paying attention. And you were. So let's go back to acting out your dream, since mine seems to have hit a snag."

"I'm not in the mood," Morgan answered stiffly.

"Oh, that's too bad," he replied, apparently not bothered by her declaration.

He slipped his hand between their bodies, back to the place he'd been stroking so sensuously before. "Are you sure you're not in the mood? You certainly feel awfully warm and damp for someone with a sudden headache," he pointed out, letting his fingers continue to caress her so she didn't stand a chance of resisting.

Of its own volition, her body tightened around his hand, and she gave up the battle she hadn't wanted to win, anyway. "Maybe I can recapture the mood if I try very hard," she admitted gruffly.

"That would be nice, because I'm sure in the mood," he whispered as he arched his hips, letting his hard, taut manhood push demandingly against her soft belly.

No longer interested in his teasing or in her retaliation, Morgan knew she wanted to make love to this man. She'd never really felt so involved before. At nineteen she'd lacked the assurance. And it hadn't taken long before she'd lost the desire to give any more of herself than necessary to a man who seemed only to take.

Kissing his neck, she breathed in his scent deeply as she tasted his warm flesh with her lips. Drawing her lips across the abrasive hairs on his neck, she lowered her head and started on a downward sensual journey. At his chest, she rubbed her face against the curly dense hair that covered the firm flesh she delighted in.

Sighing, she laid her head on the tensed muscles of his hard, flat stomach. He had stopped the intimate play of his fingers when she had moved beyond his reach, and now his hands stroked her wherever they could reach.

Brazenly she moved against him, savoring the feel of him against her soft sleekness. She slipped her hand down and captured his hardness with her tentative fingers. At her touch, a low moan escaped him.

Morgan smiled in private satisfaction and became more confident with her caresses. He was no longer interested in jokes, either. She had done it. She had this beautiful man hungry for her. She guided his velvety hard manhood up until she cradled it against the softness of her breast. When he realized what she had done, his fingers bit into her shoulders, and he arched passionately.

His blatant desire fed her own need. She had never been so desired, so wanted, so needed by a man. Riding high on her own feeling of power, she shifted her body until she was able to stroke him intimately with her lips.

"Morgan," he groaned, as he writhed under her erotic assault. Unable to take any more, Trace pulled her up, and clasping her hips, he slowly lowered her, anchoring her firmly upon him.

Sobbing with pleasure that bordered on torment, Morgan threw back her head and arched her body, driving him deeper into possession of her. In a supple, ageless dance, controlled by the hot desire that surged through her repeatedly, she drove both of them higher and higher until, with a cry, they exploded like overwound springs.

Collapsing against his damp, musky body she lay panting, relaxed and slightly dazed. As she drifted back to consciousness, the one errant thought that had been tugging at her crystallized. Lifting her head, she looked at Trace as he lay with his eyes closed, a picture of satisfied relaxation. "Steven was waiting up for you? How did he know you were coming over?"

A low moan came from the back of his throat as he opened one eye and looked at her appraisingly. "Are you sure we have to go into this now?"

"Do we have to go into it at all?" she countered, narrowing her eyes.

Sighing deeply, he pushed her head back down on his chest and held it there with a hand resting on her cheek. "Yes, unfortunately. Steven knew I was coming over because he called me at work today and asked me to talk to you." Sighing again, he twisted his body until he could reach the blankets he'd pulled off her when he'd snuck into her bed. Catching them, he covered both of them.

"Seems that Steven got into a little trouble at school." He patted her shoulder comfortingly when Morgan sighed. "Nothing all that bad, but he thought I might be able to judge his actions and present them to you in a more reasonable manner than a school official. He was going to tell you himself, but as I recall, there was something about my knowing how emotional mothers can get about little things, and since I spend so much time watching justice at work, he thought that I'd be a natural for this."

Morgan snorted in amused disgust.

"Yes, I know. But it sounded pretty reasonable when he presented it."

"You have been had, Mr. Detective, sir," she teased.

"Probably, but I was ready to use any excuse to sneak into your bed. You know, Morgan, that kid could go far," he observed respectfully.

"Yes, possibly as far as the penitentiary. So what did he do this time?"

"I don't suppose there's an easy way to say this." He took a deep breath, as if fortifying himself. "Steven has been selling lottery tickets to his classmates and to a couple of other classes." When she muttered something unintelligible and tried to bury her face in his chest, he patted her shoulder again.

"He assures me it was all on the up-and-up. For a mere fifty cents a week, those fortunate children had a chance of winning five dollars in a weekly draw, and another chance at the monthly draw for ten dollars. He's kept careful records of the winners and can prove that all the winnings have been paid out."

"Records, he kept records," Morgan groaned into his chest.

"Lots of criminals keep very tidy records. You'd be surprised," Trace told her with a hint of laughter in his voice. "Anyway, the poor kid got busted today, and you have to go see the principal tomorrow."

"He screws up and I have to go see the principal? Where's the justice in that?"

"According to your son, the old guy is mad because he didn't think of it himself. A real bad loser, that principal. He didn't even accept the cut Steven offered him," he explained dryly.

"Oh, no," Morgan whimpered. "Trace, you locked up the wrong kid. Go drag Steven off and give him the same cellmate you gave Matt. Go. Do it now." She pushed on his chest, urging him on. "Did you point out that there's a law against that type of thing?"

"Yes, ma'am. Even called it a clear-cut rackets charge, and suggested he might want to avoid the vice squad in the near future," he answered cheerfully. "However, Steven pointed out that it can't be all that bad—he's only copying the state lottery."

"Did you mention that the state can execute people too?" she asked.

"Not in Michigan it can't. Besides, I didn't want to give him any more ideas."

"Good point," she acknowledged.

Lying there with the reassuring heaviness of his arms around her, she wasn't particularly concerned about Steven. She'd go see the principal tomorrow and he'd explain that such creativity had to be channeled into a positive direction. She'd agree, come home and make

Steven come up with a fitting punishment. He always picked terribly painful things that she never would have been able to think of herself. Once, when he sold jawbreakers to his second-grade class for only a three-hundred-percent markup—the convenience of being able to buy candy instead of lunch had been his justification for the rip-off—he'd ordered himself to use all his profits to throw a class party. She'd never forget the sad child who almost burst out crying when he handed his money to the clerk at the grocery store.

"You sure keep this bed hot."

"I'm not used to sharing my bed with a furnace," she explained. "I can turn down the electric blanket if you want me to. It's probably on pretty high."

"You have an electric blanket *and* a heated water bed?" he asked in disbelief.

"I get cold." Morgan shrugged against him.

After a moment's hesitation, he asked, "How do you feel about regular, unheated beds with dual-control electric blankets?"

"Well," she drawled, "I suppose if the compensation was great enough I could live with that arrangement."

"Thank God," he muttered gratefully.

8

"WHY CAN'T I GO in with her?" Morgan asked the man in white who stood before her, blocking the door they had just wheeled Amanda through.

"They're going to take a series of head X rays, ma'am," the man explained patiently. "We don't want anyone to be unnecessarily exposed to the radiation. She'll be out in a moment, and they'll take her directly back to the exam room."

Morgan bit her lower lip hard, hoping the pain would help hold back the fear-induced hysteria that kept eating away at her self-control. It had been like this ever since she'd gotten the call from the stable manager. She wasn't completely clear about exactly what had happened, but it sounded as if the kids had raced their horses back to the stables and Amanda's mount had been too keyed up to stop at a gate. The horse had made it over the fence and so had Amanda, for that matter, just not on his back.

By the time she'd been called, Amanda was already en route to the emergency room. Dropping everything, Morgan had arrived a few moments after the ambulance, only to stand helplessly waiting for the doctors to run enough tests so they could give her some idea of Amanda's condition.

She'd never felt so ineffectual in her life. The sight of her daughter lying unconscious on the hospital gurney seemed so unreal, yet was horribly real. Morgan felt as if she'd entered a madhouse full of distorting mirrors. Nothing looked as it should—people, things, rooms, hallways were all warped, flickering, faded images that floated around a very concrete little girl who lay pale and quiet on the stainless steel table.

Somewhere in her mind it registered that she wasn't functioning all that well. People had been repeating things over and over to her, but their voices came from so far away that she had a hard time believing they were talking to her. They'd tried to give her some tranquilizers, but she was afraid to take them. She'd never had one before, and what if they made things worse?

The hospital staff had forced her to leave Amanda once before, when they'd examined her, and she'd been thinking clearly enough to use the time to call C.J. and ask him to take care of the boys. That call had been her last constructive action. If there had been something she could have done, she was sure she wouldn't be quite so dysfunctional, but there was nothing. All she could do was wait for the doctors to give her some information.

Walking very carefully, as if she were afraid some uncontrolled motion might shatter her, Morgan started back down the hall to wait for Amanda. Her eyes fixed on the door she would enter, she didn't notice the large blond man until he touched her arm.

"Morgan?" Trace questioned softly.

Morgan accepted his sudden appearance as if she had expected him. With a little whimper, she turned and walked into his arms.

"Where's Amanda?"

"They're taking head X rays. They wouldn't let me go with her. I'm supposed to wait for her in the exam room." Morgan leaned against his broad chest, letting him shelter her for a moment.

"Let's go wait for her." He carefully tucked her against his side and started walking down the hall in the direction she had been heading. "Morgan, I don't know where the exam room is. You'll have to show me," he coached her, as if she were a small, fragile child.

"Here." She pointed toward a door.

Seating her on the only chair in the room, Trace crouched beside her and held her cold delicate hands securely in his large warm ones. "What have they told you so far?"

"Nothing really," she sighed. "Amanda is still unconscious. The doctor who examined her said her reflex responses were encouraging, but they won't be able to tell much until they run some more tests. They did mention that she could regain consciousness anytime." Morgan's eyes started to overflow. "I wish they would let me go with her. What if she wakes up and gets frightened? She's still just a little girl."

"They know where you are, and they'll get you if she needs you. These people are good—they know what to do," he said, trying to reassure her.

Morgan sat silently looking at the hands covering hers. She didn't question why he was here, or how he knew about the accident. She only cared that she wasn't alone, and that she wasn't quite so overwhelmed when he was beside her.

Trace stood when the door opened and helped the nurse maneuver the gurney into the small exam room. Morgan went to her daughter and stroked the pale face she loved so much. She was only dimly aware that Trace was talking with the nurse.

"Amanda," she whispered, trying to control the burst of hope that made her hands tremble.

There, she'd seen it again. "Amanda, wake up, baby," Morgan pleaded with her daughter, focusing all her energy on the flickering eyelashes as if, by her will alone, she could force the eyes open.

"Morgan, is something happening?" Trace was at her side.

"She's moving her eyes. I think she's waking up." Morgan was unable to contain her excitement. "There. See. She did it again.

"Amanda, baby, open your eyes," Morgan pleaded once more.

As if responding to her mother's desperation, Amanda moaned softly and opened her eyes for a brief moment. "Mama," she whispered weakly, "I fell off Judd."

"I know, baby. I know." Morgan was oblivious of the tears that ran unrestrained down her cheeks.

"Could you unsaddle him and rub him down, please?" the little girl requested politely before she drifted off again.

Turning to face Trace, Morgan looked at him with emotion brimming in her eyes. "She's going to be all right now, isn't she?"

"Looks that way, love." Trace wrapped his arms around her, only to have Morgan jerk out of his embrace.

Slapping her hands over her mouth, she turned and ran to the garbage can that was in the room.

Bent over the open can, Morgan felt a damp cloth being placed in her hand. She'd done it again. Her embarrassment fought with relief over Amanda's recovery. Carefully wiping her mouth with the wet paper towel Trace had given her, she kept her eyes averted and walked over to where Amanda lay.

One of these days she would beat that stupid reflex, she promised herself as she watched her daughter's regular breathing. Not today obviously, but someday.

"Here—drink this," Trace ordered, handing her a paper cup filled with water.

"Thank you," Morgan muttered, accepting the cup.

"Morgan, you can look at me. I promise you there are worse things in the world than throwing up."

Morgan watched his hand come into her range of vision. Gently he pushed an errant strand of dark hair off Amanda's forehead. Worse things in the world for him maybe, but he hadn't just thrown up in front of someone he wanted to have hang around for a while. Her thoughts were interrupted by another moan from Amanda.

"Mama, my arm hurts," she whined, sounding like a very little girl.

"Baby, we're at the hospital now. I'll have them look at it. How do you feel other than that?" Morgan asked softly. Her arm? Maybe they were X-raying the wrong thing. That would be all right—she'd dealt with broken arms before. They weren't fun, but they didn't have her throwing up the way this head injury did.

"Okay, I guess. If I have a broken arm, do I have to go to school tomorrow?"

Smiling, Morgan looked up at Trace so relieved at this sign of normalcy that she forgot to be embarrassed. "We'll see what the doctor has to say."

MORGAN LEANED her head back on the headrest in Trace's car, giving in to the exhaustion of the long afternoon and evening. As she had suspected when Amanda had started trying to get out of going to school, she was going to be fine. Even her arm was only badly bruised. She would be spending the night in the hospital, however, so they could keep her under observation. Amanda viewed the whole experience as an adventure. A bed that she could move up and down, a milk shake for dinner, and a TV she didn't have to share. Relieved, Morgan decided she could count herself lucky if she managed to get Amanda to leave come morning.

Trace had been wonderful, she thought as she turned her head to watch the chiseled profile of the man driving. He'd asked the doctors all sorts of questions that she hadn't thought of at that moment but that she would have thought of tonight while she lay in bed worrying. He'd teased Amanda and managed to make her feel that spending the night in the hospital was a real treat. Most of all, he'd been there for her to lean on when she'd needed him. Which reminded her of a question she'd thought of earlier. "Trace, how did you find out about the accident?"

"Your brother called me," he told her.

"He did?" she responded, surprised. "I wonder why he did that?" she mused. "You don't even know C.J., do you?"

"No. I think one of the kids must have told him how to get hold of me." After a moment's hesitation, he went on. "You should have called me yourself. You had no business going to the hospital and trying to deal with that on your own."

Morgan looked at him in utter amazement. He was angry. If the way he clutched the steering wheel was any indication, he was very angry. Why would he think that she would have called him? It had taken a monumental effort to remember her brother's phone number, and she'd been phoning him for years. "It didn't even cross my mind that you would want to be involved with this."

"Of course I didn't *want* to be involved. You didn't want to be involved, either, but it was one of those things that involved you, anyway. You should have called me as soon as you'd heard that there had been an accident."

"Oh," she replied weakly.

He spun off the road so aggressively that the seat belt bit into her shoulder.

"Why are we going to your apartment? I thought you were driving me home."

"When I called your brother to tell him Amanda was all right, I told him not to expect you home tonight. He's going to spend the night with the boys." He was making a visible effort to calm down, or at least to control his temper.

"I think I should go home," Morgan replied stubbornly. After something like this she wanted to see and touch the boys, just to reassure herself that all was well.

"Too late—we're already here."

Morgan watched him resentfully as he walked around and opened her side of the car. "I would rather go home tonight, Trace. The boys might need me. This whole thing has upset them, too."

"The boys are fine. Your brother can take care of whatever comes up. Tonight I need you," he stated so bleakly that she was left speechless. Taking her arm, he led her unprotesting up the stairs to his door.

Once they'd entered the apartment, Morgan turned to him. "Trace, what's the matter?"

He avoided her eyes. "Why don't you go take a shower and then get into bed. You're exhausted."

"You needed me to go to bed with you?" she questioned skeptically. All her instincts told her that for what he was going through, sex was not the cure.

"No. I'm not sure what I need, but I doubt that it's sex. Look, I'm going to make myself a drink. Do you want one?" She looked at him with big concerned eyes as she shook her head. "Don't worry about it, kid. Go take a shower and give me a few minutes to think things out." He gave her a twisted, apologetic smile as he gently pushed her in the direction of his bathroom.

Trace watched her as she left the room, turning once to give him a concerned little smile. Walking into the kitchen, he helped himself to a stiff drink. He was a little concerned about himself, too. Since C.J.'s call, he had been operating on gut instincts. His first reaction had been disbelief, followed by a panicked need to get to Morgan and Amanda.

He knew that some people might describe him as being a hard man, and his profession hadn't stimulated the development of a soft side, but he'd never considered himself to be cold and emotionless. Now he had to wonder. The depth and range of the emotions he'd experienced in the past five hours were beyond anything he'd ever expected existed.

He needed Morgan tonight. Not so much to take care of his physical needs as his psychological. And it bothered him. She was only a lover that he'd known for a few weeks. She shouldn't be having this impact on him. With a large swallow of the amber liquid, he admitted that he just might have waited a little too long to evaluate this relationship. It was entirely possible that he was already totally lost, and he didn't even know the nature of the beasts who inhabited this particular forest.

With sudden clarity he knew what he needed from Morgan tonight.

Half an hour later, Trace slipped his naked body under the sheets beside Morgan. She immediately scooted over to his side and pressed herself as close to him as she could.

Running his hands along her body, not particularly as a lover but in the manner she thought he probably used to frisk people, he exclaimed in surprise, "You're freezing!"

"You might have warned me that you have a very limited supply of hot water," she complained. "At the very moment that I was covered with soap, ice cubes started coming out the shower head."

Trace grinned in the darkness and tucked her in against him, warming her. "It was fine this morning, but it goes on the blink regularly. Remind me to call the superintendent before I shower, please." After a few minutes, when she'd stopped shivering, he asked her seriously, "Morgan, do things like this happen often?"

"You mean do I take ice baths? Never. But if you mean do I come to bed freezing? Yes, all the time. I think I'm cold-blooded," she answered, nestling comfortably in his warm embrace.

"Not that," he corrected. "Do your kids go through these things a lot?"

"Often enough that I'll probably have gray hair by the time I'm thirty-five," she answered, not taking him seriously.

"Tell me about it."

Morgan felt a little siren go off in her head. Apparently her lover had just received an overdose of kids. She'd known it was going to happen, she thought with a sigh, she had just wanted it to take a little longer. She wasn't surprised that it had happened this quickly, however. She'd done a lousy job of keeping him isolated from the trials and tribulations of parenting. In three weeks he'd arrested Matt, intervened for Steven, run interference with her ex-husband, held her together through a mother's trauma, comforted Amanda and, for all that, they'd managed to make love only twice. Hardly sounded like the kind of thing a man such as Trace would put up with for long.

That was no surprise, but she still felt a little sad. In a very short time, he had come to mean a lot to her, and his absence would leave a big gap. Trying to look at the situation optimistically, she decided that it had been a nice three weeks, and his little interaction with Matt seemed to be having some long-term positive effects. "What do you want to know?" she asked hollowly. There was no reason to hide things. If he needed more reasons for calling it off, the least she could do was oblige him. Maybe she even owed it to him to make his task easier. He'd done a lot for her.

"Everything," he stated emphatically. "I want to know about broken bones, school problems, social problems. I want to know what you've had to deal with since you took full responsibility for your kids. We've got all night, and if the story takes that long, so be it."

So she did—she told him everything. What it felt like to be a pregnant mother at twenty with a colicky baby who routinely screamed for six and seven hours at a time. She told him about the time Matt had fallen from a tree and broken his arm, and about how Steven had broken his leg when a sled at school had crashed into him. She told about how she'd sat on her deck, chain-smoking a friend's cigarettes, while watching a fire getting closer and closer to a row of hundred-thousand-dollar homes. A fire that Matt had set when he'd been experimenting with creating rocket fuel in a dry field. She told him of the time Amanda had jumped into a pond and hadn't resurfaced until Matt found her and pulled her up, half-conscious. She told him about Steven's setting up an organization to sell copies of completed homework to classmates. Also of Matt's never-ending run-in with teachers and administrators who were threatened and confused by a kid they knew to be so much brighter than they were. She talked until her voice was raspy and every third word was punctuated with a yawn.

All the while she talked, the man at her side was silent. He would occasionally rub her back if she told him something that he seemed to think upset her, but that was it. Unable to see his face in the dark, Morgan couldn't tell what he was thinking, but it was better that way, she decided. She was trying to give him all the justification in the world to end their affair if that was what he wanted. If she could have seen a disgusted or even a pitying look she wouldn't have had the courage to have kept on talking.

This driving away of a man she liked so very much made her terribly sad, but in a way her monologue was therapeutic. Talking about her problems, even for a lousy reason like this, seemed to make them a little less formidable. Being able to say everything out loud helped put her frustration in perspective. Perhaps she should consider finding a lover every three weeks or so, she thought dryly. Ending an affair was much cheaper than going to an analyst for stress therapy. Finally talked out, Morgan lay quietly.

"Good night, lady." Trace kissed her forehead.

"Good night," Morgan answered pathetically. Good night and goodbye.

"I THOUGHT YOU PROMISED to have something better than frosted flakes the next time I came over," Morgan complained across the breakfast table.

"I didn't know you wanted something different. I thought you just didn't like the stale stuff I had last time. This is a brand-new box purchased just for you," he prevaricated, pouring milk into his own bowl.

"I meant it, Trace. I'm going to dock points from your diet history if you eat junk like this," Morgan warned.

"Diet history? Seems like you mentioned that before. Is that, by any chance, something I'm supposed to know about?" he asked, casting her a sheepish look.

"No, not yet. But you might consider coming to my lecture tomorrow when I give the assignment out. It takes the place of one exam, and since all that's left this semester is this assignment and the final, you really should start trying to get points somewhere," Morgan suggested as she ate the sugary cereal with obvious relish.

The morning had been very hard. Trace had awakened her with kisses, but once she was awake he'd booted her out of bed and hurried her through the morning, claiming that they needed to see Amanda. No time for lovemaking this morning, and she doubted that he would ever find the time again.

Swallowing her disappointment and at the same time chiding herself for feeling that way when his reaction was what she'd expected all along, she promised herself that she wouldn't let him see her hurt. A stiff upper lip and all that.

"Yeah, I guess I should do something," he agreed without enthusiasm. "Do you remember if any of my other test scores were even close to the D range?" he asked.

"The first one wasn't too far off, but the second was a total bust," Morgan told him regretfully.

"You know, I kind of liked the classes I made," he admitted. "It's just such a rotten time of day for me to arrange to be off."

"Why did you sign up for a nutrition class, anyway? Surely there were other easy classes that might have interested you more," she remarked.

"It sounded like a class that wouldn't cause any problems. My adviser swore that it was one of those famed classes that football players take. The ones where they never open a book and always get As," he said disgustedly. "I needed the credits, so I thought, 'What the heck, I'll do it.' After all, it couldn't be too hard—everyone knows how to eat."

"You sound like Matt," Morgan commented. He did, too—that easy-out attitude had gotten Matt into more than one jam. "Your adviser was right about one thing—lots of football players do take the class. But they generally take it because they're thinking about someday being coaches and they want some nutrition background. Of course, the ones that pass do tend to open books."

"Well, here's to the diet history." He lifted a glass of milk, offering a toast to the one thing that could possibly prevent his attending another semester of classes that he'd have to schedule around.

MORGAN GLANCED UP at the clock, calling over to the graduate student who was checking out the equipment that they would be needing when her young research subjects showed up. "I'll be back in a minute. I have to make a phone call."

She'd been calling Amanda every fifteen or twenty minutes since she'd left her at home. The doctors had given Amanda a clean bill of health but felt that she ought to stay quiet for the rest of the day. When Morgan had asked, they'd assured her that Amanda did not need to be watched constantly but then had given her a long list of things to watch for.

Morgan had canceled her graduate classes, but there was no way to reach the teens who were helping her in this project. When she'd left Amanda, she'd told her that she would call often and be home in an hour and a half. After showing her grad student what to do, she was planning on skipping out and letting the others handle it today.

"Amanda?" Morgan asked when she heard the phone being picked up.

"No," Trace unexpectedly answered her.

"What are you doing there? Is everything all right?" Trace had driven her back to the hospital and had gone in with her to see about getting Amanda discharged. He'd stayed through all the rigmarole and had talked to the doctor with her, but he'd made no plans to come by the house later. The last she'd seen of him, he'd checked both Amanda's and her seat belt and had told her to drive carefully.

"Everything is fine. I knew you had to be at work this afternoon, so I dropped by to keep Amanda company," he explained, not really clarifying anything.

"Oh. I'm almost finished up here. I'll be home in forty-five minutes or so."

"No hurry. I thought I'd hang around awhile, anyway. Drive carefully—the roads were starting to ice up when I came over," he warned before saying goodbye and hanging up.

That was one notable understatement, Trace thought to himself. He was planning to hang around here a very long while, if all went according to plan.

After seeing Morgan and Amanda drive off, he'd gone back to his empty apartment. Looking around the place, he'd really seen it for the first time in a long while. He had been struck by how dreary and dismal it was. No pictures, no little knickknacks with sentimental value—nothing. It was just the run-down apartment that he lived in when he wasn't at the station. The contrast between this place and Morgan's, the kids' projects proudly displayed, posters reflecting Matt's barbarian phase decorating every bare wall, notes on the bedroom doors giving warnings or instructions to someone who might want to enter, pictures of smiling kids from infancy on, and even a big lummox of a dog who thumped his tail when Trace walked in pointed out to him what an empty and lonely existence he had.

Morgan's story of her life with her family revealed the same thing. She'd had the kids too early and too closely together, but listening to her, he'd seen her life as a kaleidoscope of ever-changing effects while his own seemed to show up as a black-and-white police mug shot. Not that he felt cheated—he was content with what he'd done with his life so far, but now something brighter was being dangled in front of him.

He wanted Morgan and he wanted her family. It might be that he needed them, their warmth, the commotion that surrounded them and even their problems, he admitted to himself. He'd been looking out for only himself long enough.

The problems that had bothered him a couple of weeks ago didn't seem particularly insurmountable anymore. So Morgan was better educated than he was. It didn't seem to make any difference to her. In fact, he kind of wondered if she had ever thought about it. Besides, an education was a hard thing to evaluate. Morgan had more letters after her name than he had or ever would have, but those letters were only useful in that protected little academic world she worked in. Out in the real world, she was a little lost.

Even his lousy childhood didn't seem to enter into things much. Morgan's kids were not little tykes that he would mess up if he did something wrong. They were almost young adults, with their personalities pretty much formed. After listening to her talk last night, he knew that even if he made a lot of mistakes he could still help out.

Her life had been spent bouncing from one catastrophe to another. She kept her sense of humor about the whole thing, but she shouldn't have had to go through it alone. He'd found himself silently thanking C.J. and her mother for being there when he hadn't, but that was about to change. Now he was here and he would take care of them all. Well, at least he and Morgan could give each other support while they tried to take care of things, he amended, when he thought about how little control a person has over runaway horses or sleds or slippery tree limbs.

Walking back to the family room to read Morgan's nutrition book while Amanda watched some old movie on TV, he felt a satisfied warmth of belonging, not to just one person or to a job but to a whole family.

All he had to do was talk Morgan into agreeing with him. That thought set him back a bit. He hadn't the faintest idea how Morgan was viewing their relationship or what plans she had made for the future. Jason, his partner, was constantly warning him to run for his life. According to him, a woman with three kids would be frantic for a man and willing to do most anything to trap one into marriage. That would be convenient if it was true, but somehow he thought Jason was as wrong about this as he'd been about who was spending the night with Morgan that time he'd made a fool of himself over C.J.

If Morgan wasn't desperate for a man, he'd have to do something to make her that way. Opening his book, he gave serious consideration to unplugging the heater on her water bed. At least then she'd be desperate to sleep cuddled up beside him.

9

PLACING THE TRANSPARENCIES for the overhead projector back into the folder, Morgan looked up and smiled at Trace, who was walking down the stairs of the lecture hall toward her. At first she'd thought he'd missed another lecture because his regular seat was empty, but then she'd noticed him sitting up in a back corner.

"Glad to see you could make it, Detective," she greeted the frowning man.

"It will be the last time I do, if you don't do something to control those kids." He cast a frustrated look over his shoulder to a group of young women standing by the door. He took Morgan's lecture material out of her hands, and they fell into step together.

"What's the matter? Did your fan club find you hidden way up in the back?" she inquired, perhaps overly sympathetically.

"It's not funny. If they get any worse I'm going to arrest them for soliciting." He ran his hand through his hair.

"They'd like that."

"Oh?"

"If my arrest was a sample of your standard arrest procedure, then I'd say it was exactly what they had in mind," she teased, opening the lecture room door for him.

"Not cute." He looked down at her out of the corner of his eye. "I'm serious, Morgan. Make them stop. It's embarrassing."

"It's not my problem. You're the one with the sex appeal." Suddenly snapping her fingers, she looked up at him. "Why don't you try throwing up. That almost always works for me."

"Thanks a million. Any other ideas, Doctor?" he drawled, shortening his stride a bit so she could keep up with him without trotting.

"Bring some guy to class and put your arm around him?" she suggested, her eyes flashing with laughter.

"Funny lady." Reaching her office door, he turned and cuffed her playfully on the side of the head.

His play carried not the slightest hint of violence. The large palm pushing her cheek was really a friendly caress, but when Morgan heard the feminine gasp of outrage and looked into the horrified eyes of the department secretary who stood staring at Trace as if he were a monster, she knew that it hadn't looked like a love touch.

"Good morning," Morgan smiled weakly at the very proper woman who was planning on retiring at the end of the year.

"Oh, dear!" the older woman exclaimed. Scuttling off to the office, she cast a worried look over her shoulder at Trace.

"Did I do it again?" Trace studied the retreating woman's back.

"Probably, but don't plan on seeing the department head about it. When news of your vicious attack gets around, I'm afraid they'll lock the doors," Morgan informed him gravely.

Trace shook his head disgustedly. "I've had enough of this maligning of my sterling character." Bending down, he kissed her lightly on the cheek, handed her the notes and walked away. "See you tonight," he called over his shoulder.

"Tonight?" Morgan echoed quietly, watching his broad back disappear down the hall. Although she'd given it a great deal of thought, she had no way of knowing exactly how, or even if, he was going to wind down their short affair. She'd finally decided to play it by ear. When he'd come over yesterday and kept Amanda company, she'd assumed it was a nice goodbye gesture to the little girl, especially when he'd left for work the moment Morgan had walked in the door. Today if he had been distant to her, she was set to assume her teacher's role, but it looked as if he was going to disengage himself by playing the good buddy. If he wanted a buddy she'd be it, just for the sake of a little more of his company. And if she was wrong and he hadn't been scared off . . . she was game.

"LOOK, IT'S AMANDA'S night for dinner. If you don't want to eat what she cooks, then make yourself a sandwich, but please spare us your complaints!" Morgan yelled from the family room where she was studying the bedding section of the phone book.

"Is somebody going to get that door?" she called when the bell rang a second time.

"Never mind," Trace called out. "I let myself in."

Morgan watched the tawny-haired man toss a bag on the table, walk over to the couch and flop down beside her. "Are you going to yell about the door being unlocked?"

"No, I've given up on that. I'll have to come up with some other way of making you lock it," he answered amiably, putting his arm over her shoulders and kissing her a brief hello.

"Were we supposed to have a date or something tonight?" Morgan snuggled in close to his side.

"Not that I know of. I just brought my stuff over. Thought I might as well get started."

Morgan tilted her head and looked at him suspiciously. "Do I know what you're talking about?"

"Sure, it was your idea. I have to admit it makes sense—I do need the points." He flashed her a smile a late-night used car dealer would envy.

"What makes sense?" She was becoming very uneasy. This had all signs of a walk down the primrose path. It wasn't as if she didn't trust him, Morgan assured herself, she'd trust him with her life.

"Why, moving in with you for the three days I have to do that diet history." Lifting his feet, he put them on the coffee table.

Sitting up straight, Morgan shoved his arm off. "Let me see if I have this correct. You're considering moving in here for three days until your assignment is completed."

"You know, it used to really irritate me when you did that, but now I think your professor act is kind of cute."

He leaned away from her as if to get a better view of the show she was putting on.

"You may not move in here," she stated emphatically.

"Why not, Doctor?" he asked, draping his arm back around her shoulders and pulling her over to him, ignoring the fact that she was holding herself so stiffly that she leaned awkwardly against him.

"The kids."

"What about us?" Matt asked from behind them.

"Hi." Trace turned his head to acknowledge the two boys who had just entered the room. "I'm going to move in for three days while I complete the diet history your mother assigned the class. She says I can't because you all will be scandalized."

"A diet history, huh?" Matt looked thoughtful. "Is that the one where you have to write down everything you eat and then analyze it for calories, vitamins and stuff like that?"

"That's the one," Trace confirmed.

"She made us do that once." Matt's displeasure with the task showed clearly. "It's not too bad if you set the situation up right. I'll help you calculate your caloric requirements. I made up a program that does it all, Amanda cooks tonight, and all she ever does is open packages, so that will be a breeze."

Noting Trace's questioning look, Steven took over. "If it's out of a box, you just look on the back of the package and copy the nutritional info. That way you don't have to look up everything you eat in a book."

"Tomorrow night Steven cooks," Matt resumed. "For a price, maybe he'll open boxes, too."

"For you, I'll do it free," Steven offered magnanimously, beaming happily at his own generosity. "But Mom cooks the next night, and she never opens packages," he warned grimly.

A moment of thoughtful silence descended on the group. Morgan's low groan was all that was heard. "I got it! Order pizza. Mom's got this whole list of junk-food breakdowns. You won't have to even open a book," Matt explained excitedly, obviously pleased with his solution.

"Well, now that that's taken care of, do you want us to carry in a suitcase or anything?" Steven asked.

"Sure, it's in my trunk." He dug his keys out of his pocket and tossed them to the boys.

After the boys had piled out of the house with their usual noise, Trace patted Morgan on the back consolingly. "You know, I can see how living with a genius and a hustler can have its advantages. You just told me the rotten parts the other night," he said accusingly.

Morgan leaned her head back and looked at the ceiling, obviously seeking divine counsel.

A moment later Matt came into the house carrying a suitcase. "Do you want me to put this in Mom's room?" he yelled from the front door, causing his mother to sigh deeply.

"No, put it in the study!" Trace yelled back.

Morgan opened one eye and looked up at Trace. Slowly a slightly malicious smile broke through and she lifted her head. "Matt, where is your brother?"

"Uh, well, umm, he kind of thought he'd hang around outside awhile," the boy stammered before taking off rapidly down the hall to the study.

Noting Morgan's smug expression, Trace looked a little wary. "Okay, I give. What's up with the dynamic duo?"

"Did you by any chance leave those handcuffs in the glove compartment?" She nonchalantly twisted a long strand of her hair around her finger.

Morgan watched as the questioning look in his eyes turned to one of comprehension. "He wouldn't. Would he?" Seeing the answer in the way she looked at him, he gave her a twisted grin. "That puts me in my place, I guess. How long do we leave him captive?"

"Not long—it's only about fifteen degrees or so out there," she answered regretfully.

Grunting his agreement, Trace stood up.

"Lots of advantages, lots and lots and lots of them." Morgan tossed his own words back at him cheerfully as he started down the hall to get the handcuff keys from Matt and then see about liberating Steven from whatever he was shackled to.

When he had disappeared, Morgan leaned back on the couch. Three days. He wanted to spend three days with her and her family, and the kids didn't seem to mind in the least. A smile came unbidden to her face. She sat up and started calling bedding stores to see who could make a quick delivery, no longer even bothering to ask about the price.

MORGAN WATCHED the people sitting around the table and fought her impulse to laugh. Since she'd given Trace the assignment, she was destined to play the villain of the piece, and playing the chuckling scoundrel seemed to lessen the significance of the important business being conducted. Trace, however, took full points for putting up with the nonsense, she thought appreciatively. After all, it was his stomach that was being ruined.

While the rest of them had nice normal-looking spaghetti, Trace had agreed to a huge serving of noodles accompanied by a minute amount of sauce. It had something to do with the portion sizes on the various packages. The real killer was the whole can of applesauce that he was ordered to eat by Amanda, who seemed to think that dividing by two or three was too burdensome a task even to consider. This lovely meal was accompanied by two pieces of plain bread, water and a can of pudding usually reserved for school lunches. Another meal like this and she'd be willing to bet that he'd beg to be allowed to open a book.

Happening to catch Trace's eye, she hastily bit her lip to hold back the laughter. He was so good with the kids. Moaning and groaning good-naturedly about their imposed sanctions, he seemed to fit in as if he had always lived here. Morgan could hardly believe her good luck in finding this man. At the rate he was going, this little experiment to improve the quality of her love life might go on for quite a while.

She hoped so. She very much hoped so, but there was an obnoxious little voice inside her that kept telling her she was kidding herself. What was going on tonight was a bona fide family-of-five-type dinner. That was just too many. Something would have to give and Trace would walk out. It might not even be the family situation that drove him off. It might well be her. What did she know about developing a relationship with a man?

One failed marriage when she was almost a child and maybe a dozen real dates. Hardly enough experience to let her captivate a man like this one.

"Do you suppose they've all finally gone to bed?" Trace asked in a conspirator's whisper as he sat on the couch beside her hours later.

"More than likely. Why? Did you have something in mind for tonight that didn't include them?" Morgan asked seductively.

"Yes, something that definitely does not include your kids," he growled in her ear, nipping at her lobe.

"Oh, yeah. What, pray tell?" She turned toward him and slid her arms around his neck.

"This." He started to plant little kisses on her mouth. "And this," he whispered as he sucked her lower lip between his teeth and caressed it with his tongue. "And this." He covered her lips with his and proceeded to turn her world into a warm, fuzzy place dominated by his gently exploring tongue. Drawing back slightly, he breathed a sigh into her. "But mostly I wanted to sneak out into the kitchen and make myself a sandwich."

"A sandwich?" she repeated, blinking owlishly at him.

"A sandwich. Morgan, I'm starving. I'm a big guy, and I burn up all those calories chasing down the bad guys. I can't live on a plate of noodles," he explained, setting her upright on the couch.

"Don't forget the applesauce. You had a lot of applesauce," she reminded him.

"Yeah, lots and lots of applesauce," he agreed dryly. "Come on, lady, duty calls." He rose to his feet, swinging her along with him. "You'll have to come with me so in case one of the kids catches me I can claim you're the one eating the sandwich."

"Boy, you're a great law-and-order role model," Morgan chided him.

"Does that bother you?" he asked with a tension that he couldn't fully mask.

"Does what bother me?" Morgan took the things to make his dinner out of the refrigerator. There was no missing the careful control in his voice. But she also thought she detected a bit of defensiveness, as if he were being threatened.

"That I'm not as educated as you are," he said emotionlessly.

Morgan looked up from the sandwich she was creating. He looked harder now than she had ever seen him, and this time it was not an act. He was braced and waiting for a blow. Somehow he looked vulnerable and dangerous at the same time, like a wounded animal still powerful enough to make a last stand, taking some of his enemies with him. What she wanted to do was to walk over to him, wrap her arms around him and tell him that whatever it was that was hurting him she would make it all right. She didn't, though. She'd had enough experience with pained males to know that after the age of six or seven sympathy wasn't what they were looking for.

Turning her attention back to the sandwich, she started slicing the cheese. "I was married to a man who is considered to be extremely well educated. He's widely published and quite respected by others in his field. His great education doesn't mean a thing when it comes down to human relationships. It doesn't stop him from using people; it doesn't keep him honest and it doesn't make his children respect or even like him. My father and C.J. have only high school diplomas and they're both good solid people. So what's an education?" She shrugged, still keeping her eyes on the job in front of her.

"As I see it, it's just one way to get the job you want. You have a different job than I do. And frankly, I suspect that if you really wanted to do my job, you could, but I doubt very much that I could ever do yours. Do you want to be brave and eat this in here, or would you rather sneak it into the bedroom and hide?" she asked, handing him the plate holding a huge sandwich.

"Thanks," he answered in such a way that both of them knew he wasn't thanking her for the food alone. "Let's go roll around on that thing you call a bed."

After trying to brace himself up with pillows, Trace gave up on her wishy-washy bed, as he called it, and sat on the floor, leaning against the wooden frame while he ate. On the water bed, Morgan lay on her belly, hanging her head over his shoulder and harassing him about his diet.

"Even as we lie here I can hear your bones crying out, 'Help, calcium, I need calcium,'" Morgan wailed quietly in imitation of the pitiful bones.

"Your hearing's bad, Prof. That's not what my bones are yelling. I'll tell you what you're really hearing." He put down his empty plate and jumped on the bed beside her. Rolling her onto her back, he lay with a thigh draped heavily over her. "'Trace,' they're yelling. 'Bones, man, bones. Jump her bones.'" He slid over so he was directly on top of her and pushed her deeply into the bed. "And I never disregard any of my body's requests, no matter how trivial."

"Trivial!" She slapped him playfully on his shoulder. "How dare you, sir."

"I never disregard any of my body's requests, no matter how significant." He amended teasingly.

"Better, better. Not perfect, but you're showing a marked improvement." She leaned her head back in response to the little butterfly kisses he was placing near her mouth.

Morgan smiled happily to herself and lifted her hands to play in the dense hair on his head. She liked this man so much. "I'm so glad you didn't decide you couldn't take any more of us," Morgan told him thoughtlessly.

"What?" He lifted his head up and looked at her.

"Oh, nothing," she tried to backtrack, quickly realizing what she'd brought up.

"Do you mean 'us' as in you and me, or as in you and the kids?" he asked.

He hadn't moved, but Morgan was definitely under the impression that the weight resting on her, which a moment ago felt like a warm intimate caress, was now a force holding her captive. She and her big mouth.

"I didn't really mean anything. I was just talking. You know, nothing important."

He didn't bother to respond. He waited, pinning her down, and watched her expectantly.

She'd done it again. If she wasn't bursting into tears or getting into a jealous tizzy at his jokes, she was opening her big mouth and inserting her foot. At this rate she'd never get lovemaking down to the fine art she wanted to.

"Oh, all right," she conceded ungraciously. "The other night when you wanted to know all about the problems I'd had with my children, I sort of thought that you were looking for reasons to get uninvolved with me." Morgan turned her head so she didn't have to look at him. One of these days she was going to have to sweep the cobwebs off the ceiling.

"Why would I do that?" he asked, his voice emotionless.

"Will you stop questioning me as if you're the cop and I'm the criminal," she complained gruffly, meaning it. Other people had conversations—not this man. The moment he wanted information he assumed his professional demeanor, intended to wring the truth out of murderers. That technique was clearly overkill with Morgan.

"Yes, ma'am," he agreed obligingly. "So tell me why I should end this before it's even really started?"

"Could you let me up?" She tried to twist away.

"No. Answer me, Morgan, or I'll make you look at me as well as tell me what I want to know," he threatened with a hint of amusement.

Morgan let out an audible breath between her clenched teeth. "You might have noticed that my children seem to be a bit involved in our relationship. Since children are not generally considered to be much of a drawing card in an affair, I sort of thought that you might want out of the whole thing, especially after Amanda's accident."

After a long moment of silence, he drawled, "You're right. Children don't have much of a place in an affair.

I don't think I could handle an affair that had kids involved in it."

Morgan closed her eyes. What was he telling her? That she had to choose between him and her kids? Even if she managed one day to acquire a lot of experience with men, she was beginning to suspect that this one would always remain beyond her understanding. "Well, my kids do seem to be involved. Do you want to call the whole thing off?"

"No," he snapped. "Well, in a way I guess I do," he added thoughtfully.

When her chin started to tremble, Morgan quickly bit the inside of her cheeks. She would not cry. Not again. At least not until he was gone.

"I want to end the affair and start a marriage."

"What?" she blurted out, opening her eyes and turning her head to look at him. Married, he wanted to get married? To her? Was he crazy? She couldn't get married—she had responsibilities.

"You heard me. I don't think an affair is good for kids. They need something more stable than that. I want to get married. Soon," he added, as if he'd just thought of it.

No mention of love. He wanted to marry her because of her children. This had to be the most ironic situation she had ever heard of. She'd been so sure her kids had driven him away.

Once before she had agreed to a marriage because of a child. She wasn't about to do it again, she told herself, trying to ignore both the little voice that told her to go ahead and do it, and the one that kept telling her that he didn't love her. "I don't think that's a good idea."

"Why? Do you still love your ex-husband?" he grated harshly.

This conversation was getting crazier and crazier. Simon? Trace had seen the fool. "No, of course not."

"Are you sure? I saw the way you acted around him. You hate him and you've been divorced for years. I can't think of much besides unrequited love that would make you maintain that intense an emotion for that long. You're not the type to carry a grudge."

There was a heavy stillness about him that made Morgan want to clear the matter up and leave him without one solitary shred of doubt. "Yes, I hate him, and I'll probably hate him for the rest of my life. Not so much because of the marriage or divorce, but because he tried to take my kids from me a couple of years ago."

"He what?" Trace lay totally motionless, and Morgan realized again that this was a very aggressive, very protective man.

"He took me to court and tried to have me declared an unfit mother so he could get custody of the children," she explained calmly. In the face of Trace's rage, she had an instinctive urge to soothe him, calm him down before something—she didn't even try to guess what—happened.

"How could he call you unfit?" His voice was tightly controlled and still making her nervous.

"By telling a bunch of lies. Most of the charges cited were neglect, but Simon hinted at some physical abuse, too." Morgan remembered his terrifying innuendos as if the hearing were yesterday. "He's such a smooth talker. He took unrelated incidents and skillfully painted a picture that had no resemblance to the truth.

At first I couldn't believe Simon would tell such blatant lies, but what he said sounded so convincing that I was sure everyone else in the room believed him. When it was my turn, I was hardly coherent. Fortunately my lawyer believed me implicitly and worked long and hard to ferret out the truth. In the end the judge ripped into Simon, pointing out that a man who lived two miles from his children and visited them fewer than four times a year for the past five years had no business implying neglect. He ended up telling Simon that he was lucky he wasn't getting nailed with a contempt of court citation."

"If he can't tolerate being around Matt for twenty minutes, why did he even want them?" the tense man asked.

Morgan gave a short, bitter laugh and started to stroke his neck and shoulders, comforting herself as well as him. "Because of Matt. You see, in some academic circles a documented genius is far more valuable, statuswise, than a big house or racy car is in other circles. Simon had remarried, and they decided that they wanted Matt as kind of an ongoing show-and-tell to impress people. So you see, I do not have any love mixed up with the very intense hatred I have for the man."

"Guess not," he conceded. "If that's not an issue, then why won't you marry me?"

"Yesterday I didn't even think I would see you again, and now you're telling me we should marry? I can't work that fast," she answered, very much out of her depth. Wasn't there supposed to be some kind of buildup to a proposal that gave you time to marshal your defenses?

"Get off it, Morgan. You know me well enough in the important things, but if it makes you feel better I'll give you a résumé. Do you love me?" he asked without warning.

"Probab—" She stopped herself before she finished. Yes, she might very well love him. She certainly hadn't felt this way toward any other man, but she'd been fooled by love before. There was always the possibility that what she was feeling was the thirty-year-old version of the lust that had gotten her married the first time. "That's an unfair question."

"It might be, but at least I got the answer I wanted." His smug smile did nothing to reassure her, but it did let her know that he had understood her uncompleted word perfectly well.

"I'm not marrying you. At least not for a long time."

"We'll see about that. You need me, Morgan. You know you do."

"So what?" she challenged childishly. What had started out as lovemaking had turned into an emotional roller coaster ride, and she was rapidly becoming out of control. "What about my kids? You get along very well with them now, but that is only because of the novelty of it all. What happens when you get tired of the constant wear and tear of keeping up with three kids?" She flung the words at him angrily, unclear exactly who she was angry at and not willing to even ask herself the question.

"I want your children, Morgan, just like I want you. I'm not going to get tired of them. I can't guarantee that we will always get along or that there isn't going to be some resentment when we marry—"

"If we marry," she interrupted.

"When we get married," he emphasized. "But we can work it out. I'm not going to run when things get tricky."

"I don't want to get married," Morgan wailed, giving up her defiance. "Why can't we just be lovers? I've been married. Marriage isn't so great, believe me. It's a highly overrated institution. Let's be lovers. It's got to be better than being married."

"No, I don't want that. I want to be a real part of your world, not on the sidelines. Face it, Morgan, you're going to have to take the chance and risk your safe little existence. I want in, lady, and you need me in," he stated with a certainty that made her blood run cold. Grabbing her chin, he kissed her. A hard, demanding, possessive kiss that repeated on a primal level the same message his words had, and made her chances of defying him seem even more remote.

Pulling his head back, he slid away and onto his feet. "I'll give you a résumé in the morning." He started walking to the door.

"Wait a minute. Aren't you going to sleep with me?" At the very least she'd expected some grand seduction to show her exactly how badly she needed him.

"No. It would be a bad example for the kids. Besides, I won't sleep with someone who doesn't trust me," he told her quietly before closing her bedroom door.

10

"HEY, TEACH!" Trace called from down the hall. "I have to talk with you about the grade you gave me on that diet history."

"Come up to my office after class, and we can argue about it then. I'll warn you, though, I never change grades," she told him with a smile when he'd caught up with her. It had been three weeks since he had proposed. Three very disturbing weeks. He'd lived in her home until the diet history had been completed, and then he'd sort of moved out. "Sort of"—that was the key phrase. When he wasn't there for dinner, the kids wanted to know why, and two weeks ago Steven had reworked the dinner-and-dishes chart to make sure Trace did his share.

He was practically living in her pocket, and she was about to start beating down the walls in frustration. Since he had decided that they needed to set a good example for the kids, he'd refused to sleep with her. Determined to ignore the hot rush of longing that overtook her at strange times, such as when he stood up from the dinner table, or sat beside her on the couch to read the papers, she'd forced herself to pretend he was just another brother.

Her plan hadn't been a roaring success, but it had helped until he'd caught wind of what she was up to.

His retaliation was to become very unbrotherly. His large warm hand would rest possessively on her hip while he dug silverware out of the drawer beside where she stood cooking. Nor did it seem that he was able to do little things like passing the salt shaker without capturing her fingers for a brief tantalizing caress. Worst was the sadistic pleasure he took in kissing her—little kisses he snatched here and there, and long, involved, passionate ones that left her head spinning and her body aching when he said good-night at the front door. If the point of his plan was to drive her crazy, then it was working quite well.

Her plans, on the other hand, had all been dismal failures. At first she'd tried to fight fire with fire and managed to find enough reasons to touch him that she'd embarrassed herself. The only response she'd gotten from him was a knowing smile that infuriated her.

She was about to start climbing walls, and he wasn't the least bothered. The only things of a sexual nature that seemed to be getting to him were his groupies who had intensified their pursuit as the end of the semester approached.

His fan club didn't represent the only kids thrilled by the man. Her own welcomed him like a long-lost father. At first she'd tried to warn them that Trace was not a permanent member of their family and that he would one day leave. They had not accepted her wisdom graciously.

Eventually she realized that even though what she said was true, it was her own jealousy that insisted she make such a big deal about it. She'd been the most important person in her children's life up until now, and it wasn't easy knowing that Trace and the boys had spent the evening down in the basement talking men things. Every explosion of laughter seemed to grate on her nerves until she had made a determined effort to stem her jealousy.

When forced to be honest with herself, she knew she was having second thoughts about her decision to decline his proposal. She certainly knew him well enough now. She knew he left his shoes lying around wherever he took them off, and that he never put the cap back on the toothpaste, and that he moved through the house with a powerful grace that made her hungry for his touch.

The question of his sincerity about wanting to be part of her family had been answered, too. The résumé that he'd handed her the morning after he'd proposed had explained a lot. It had been a list of what he'd done in his life in chronological order. Of course there had been no insight into what it had felt like to be without any family at all. She'd cried a bit when she'd read it, but she understood things better.

It wasn't hard to believe that a man would crave a family. C.J. had practically lived with them when he'd been pressured into that trial separation. His apartment was too quiet and too lonely for him to tolerate being alone there for more than a few nights a week. Thank goodness his wife now looked as if she were willing to try to work things out. C.J. needed his family, and maybe Trace felt the same way about hers.

Although she was considering marriage, there were still some problems with Trace's proposal. A big one was that he still had not told her that he loved her. She thought that maybe he did, but she didn't know for sure. The absence of such a declaration made a gigantic gap in a marriage proposal.

Her kids were still an issue, too. Could this man, who had never really been a part of a family, stand the constant noise, mess, confusion and general craziness an active family created? So far he seemed to enjoy them, but for how long? Kids were the major cause of divorce in second marriages, and she came fully equipped with a lifetime supply of them.

Sighing to herself, Morgan put her thoughts on hold and began lecturing to her class.

"I THOUGHT YOU WERE GOING to come see me after class," Morgan remarked to the man who walked unannounced into her bedroom, where she was making her bed. He no longer complained about the door being unlocked. In fact, he took full advantage of it by making himself at home. That was another thing that was driving her crazy. She'd walk out of a shower, dripping wet hair, no makeup, ratty robe, to find him lying on her new "real" bed, reading. Or she'd be thinking about him and turn away from the sink to crash into him. There was no way she could keep the door locked, but maybe a bell around his neck would have helped.

"I was, but something came up," he answered, going around to the side of the bed opposite her and pulling the sheet up.

"What did you want to argue about?" She waited for him to straighten the blankets on his side.

"Wait until we get the bed made," he ordered, fluffing up her pillows.

Carefully tucking the bedspread under the pillows, Trace stood back and admired his work. Morgan smiled at his look of satisfaction at the neat bed. He really did seem to enjoy little domestic niceties. She wasn't the least prepared when he took a flying leap across the bed and pulled her down on it. Rolling her over to the middle of the bed, he settled his body on hers possessively.

"Now I have you in the right position to argue about my grade," he told her between kisses. Pulling his diet history out of his back pocket, he spread it out above her head on the bed.

"Trace, let me up. I can't act like a teacher when you're squashing the very life out of me," Morgan complained halfheartedly.

"Hush, you know you love it." He flipped through the pages of his assignment. "All right, now why did you give me only two points on question twelve?"

"Which one was that?" And to think that only a few weeks ago she'd considered notes from mothers to be one of the most inappropriate ways for students to try to change their grades.

"'What could you do to improve your dietary intake?'" he read. "I gave you an excellent answer. I deserved ten points at least," he growled, lowering his head to run the tip of his tongue along her lips, outlining them.

"That was a terrible answer. You're lucky that I didn't dock extra points," she defended herself.

"What do you mean terrible? It was great. 'Marry a professor of nutritional science who has three kids and let her take charge of my care and feeding,'" he quoted from his paper.

Morgan fought to keep down the laughter that was about to erupt so she could act like a professor for him. She had to agree. If she married him his diet would definitely improve. It was his sanity she questioned surviving the transition from single male to family man in one fell swoop.

"Honey?" a woman's voice came from the hallway.

"Move. Get off me," Morgan hissed frantically to Trace whose only response was to turn his head curiously toward the open bedroom door.

"Oh, I'm sorry," the soft-looking older woman apologized before turning to walk out.

"You must be Morgan's mother," Trace said, stopping her retreat.

"How could you tell?" Her mother turned back to them and looked at the man who was lifting himself off her blushing daughter.

"Your blond hair," he said dryly. "I've learned to expect blond hair from Morgan's relatives." He walked over to her and offered his hand.

"And you must be Trace," her mother identified him, shaking his hand. "Morgan, dear, you really should introduce me to your friend, but I can see that you're still mortified at being caught in such a compromising position, so I'll let it pass this time." She chattered cheerfully, ignoring the daggers her daughter was shooting at her. "I've heard so many good things about you, from the children, C.J. and Ross, and even Morgan gets a fond look in her eyes when you're mentioned."

"You heard good things about me from Ross?" Trace questioned, not believing it for one minute.

"Well, no, but you have to understand that if Ross approved of you I'd have really worried. After all, the man still likes Simon." She shook her head in obvious disbelief. "Ross is a good man, a fine father, bright, hardworking, and I love the boy, but somewhere along the line I must have made a mistake. Firstborns are rather like the first waffle you cook—they never turn out quite right." She sighed and then smiled again at Trace, who stood looking at her with bemusement. "Well, I just came to pick up the special drill bit C.J. said he needed. Those children of yours, Morgan, have been unmercifully hounding me to put in a dead bolt, and C.J. said he'd do it tonight."

"Isn't C.J. the one who put in your dead bolt?" Trace asked the silent Morgan.

"Yes," she answered tersely.

"Tell you what, why don't I go with you and give C.J. a hand? I've been meaning to talk with him, anyway," he lied.

"Did C.J. make a mess out of the lock he put in for you, Morgan?" her mother asked. When Morgan nodded, she tsked. "Well, his heart's in the right place, and usually he's pretty handy. I would be delighted to have you come over, Trace. Why don't you stay for dinner?"

"Am I invited, too?" Morgan asked, feeling the need to be with Trace if he was going to be around her mother. She had no idea whom she was protecting from whom, or even what she could do to stop her mother from making the worst possible comments. At least she could sit on the baby books if it looked as if Trace was going to be treated to a month-by-month history of her life.

"No, dear, we'll do much better without you." Her mother smiled at her in dismissal as she took the arm Trace offered and they walked out the door.

IT WAS FROM THAT MOMENT on that Morgan began to see her mother's fine touch in the campaign to talk Morgan into a marriage she was leery about.

Trace, for all practical purposes, had moved in with them again. He was back to spending the night, sleeping either on the sofa or the Hide-a-bed in the den. Mr. Law and Order himself, always setting the good example, Morgan thought caustically as she slammed the phone down. Some afternoons she felt like his secretary, taking messages to pass on to him. He must have handed out her phone number to everyone he knew.

He was living in her house, eating her food and lately even tossing his dirty clothes down the laundry chute. And what was she getting for this unoffered generosity on her part? Nothing. Not one darned thing.

She could watch him eat dinner, and he made it a point of creeping into her bedroom at night to disturb her sleep with a good-night kiss. One kiss and then he'd leave. Aside from those brief times, she hardly saw him. For this she slept in a bed that was never warm enough.

She rarely saw him because he was with the kids. Father-and-son Christmas dinners that C.J. or Gramps were usually recruited for, a Girl Scout dinner with Amanda, shopping trips that didn't include her and a trip to watch some performing horses that they'd all assumed she wouldn't be interested in seeing. You name it and he was taking the kids to it. He knew more about what was happening with her children than she did. Last week she'd tried to pin him down about the length of his stay, but he'd glanced at his watch apologetically and said that he had to run—Amanda needed to be picked up at the stables. She'd thought Amanda had been in her room reading.

The man was supposed to be her lover, not the children's nanny. She'd once claimed not to know the rules for an affair, but she could have written a better script than the one he was following.

Folding the last of his T-shirts into a neat pile, Morgan decided to have it out with him even if she needed to use his handcuffs to keep him still. Filled with determination, she gathered up his clothes and marched into the den that he'd taken over. She knocked, and at his command to enter, did, only to stop dead in her tracks.

"You're packing? Why?" She wanted something to give but not this. He wasn't supposed to leave, she thought as she felt the bottom drop out of her stomach.

"Don't look so stricken, love." He gave her a twisted smile as he took the T-shirts from her suddenly numb hands. "I decided that I needed to move back to the apartment. After all, that's where I pay rent," he joked weakly.

"Oh, I see," she said numbly.

"No, I don't think you do see. Morgan, I am not changing my mind, and I haven't gotten tired of you or the kids, so stop telling yourself that you were right all along. That you knew I couldn't hack it." He dumped the shirts on the bed and returned to her, grabbing her shoulders. "I want to live here. I want to be a part of your family, but most of all I want you." He shook her gently. "Do you hear me? I love you and I want you to be my wife."

"I'm so scared," she whispered, admitting for the first time to herself why she couldn't agree to the marriage.

"I know you are. I know," he said gently and pulled her into his arms, holding her tightly. "I wish I could make it all better for you but I can't. Only you can do that."

He held her securely for a moment and then pulled back a few inches. As he looked deeply into her eyes, a tiny groan escaped from the back of his throat. "Oh, Morgan," he sighed as he bent and took her lips.

Morgan was sure he meant to give her a light goodbye kiss, but the cold panic that chilled her heart insisted that she not let him escape. It was as if she recognized that when he walked out, he would be taking a large part of her soul. Throwing her arms around his neck, she arched her body against his and used her tongue to plunder the secrets of his sensitive mouth.

Her aggression seemed to unleash him. Tightening his arms around her, he pulled her against the hard wall of his chest. Driving his tongue past hers, he dominated the kiss. He tightened his arms until they were like steel bands holding her and then leaned forward beyond the point where she could maintain her balance.

As her feet slid between his legs, she let her body go flaccid. Her only sign of protest against his dominance was a small whimper that she didn't even know was hers. With a growl of male satisfaction, he lowered both of them to the floor, until he lay atop her, not once breaking the kiss or lessening the pressure of his arms.

His hands moved quickly over her body, pulling her clothes until Morgan felt the cold air against her skin.

Trace hesitated a moment and drank in the sight of her. "Oh, Morgan," he sighed, lowering his mouth to capture her breast. His gentle caress filled her with delicious sensations.

Rocking under the waves of desire that shook her, Morgan cried out to him. She needed this man—she needed him now. She pulled on his shoulders.

Understanding her plea, Trace raised himself a few inches and started working his pants off. They didn't make it any farther than his knees, because as soon as Morgan felt the steel silk of his manhood brush against her, she wrapped her legs tightly around the small of his back and raised herself up to him.

With a deep growl of pure male hunger, he drove himself deeply into the woman who needed him so fiercely.

Replying with a cry that echoed his, Morgan let herself be carried away in the slow, powerful, all-consuming rhythm he established. Higher and higher he took her, until with a shuddering convulsion she left all reality behind.

Floating up from the warm, sensual fog created by their lovemaking, Morgan first became aware of the cold floor she lay on. The second thing she noticed was the sounds of her children in the kitchen. "Trace, move off me," she whispered to the man who lay on her as if dead. "Trace," she urged quietly, as if whispering could prevent them from being discovered.

"Huh?" He still seemed dazed.

"Move off me. The door's not locked." When he didn't stir, she prodded him in the ribs. "The kids." That seemed to get through to him. With a sudden fluid motion he left her and locked the door.

Adjusting to the loss of his comforting weight, Morgan lay where she was and watched him fasten his belt. He was leaving. She could hardly believe it. She didn't want to believe it. The pain she felt must have been reflected in her eyes, because he bent and pulled her upright. Gently he started dressing her, as if she was a small child.

"Do you have to go?" she asked, swallowing hard as his large fingers worked on the small buttons of her blouse.

"Yes." His lips took on a grim line. "I have to go. I've been here too long as it is. Morgan, until you come to a decision, it's not fair to you, the kids, or even me for us to go on pretending we're a family."

Morgan nodded unhappily.

"I'm going to leave now." He brushed her dark hair back from her face.

"Aren't you going to finish packing?"

"No, I'll get my things some other time. I have to get out of here now, or I'll never go. Say goodbye now, Morgan. I'm going to tell the kids I'm leaving for a while. It will be hard enough as it is, but impossible if you're there watching me like that." He kissed her eyes closed. "Do whatever you need to do to think this thing through, but remember, Morgan, I love you. Don't forget that." He turned and started walking away. When he reached the door he turned and added cryptically,

"You know, lady, before I met you I used to do a pretty good job of protecting myself." He shook his head. "Take care of yourself, love."

"MOM, TRACE SAID HE WAS leaving for a while. Do you know if he'll be back for dinner?" Amanda asked her mother when Morgan finally emerged from the den where she'd spent the rest of the afternoon working on a book chapter and crying.

"No, he's not going to be eating with us for a while," Morgan answered. She didn't doubt that he had made himself clear to the kids—they just hadn't wanted to believe him, so they would go on asking various people about it until they got the answer they wanted.

"Why did he go?" Matt asked defiantly. "Was he mad about what I said the other night about cops thinking they're better than everyone else?"

Morgan tightened her lips unconsciously. This was a little like going through a divorce. The kids were going to blame themselves for Trace's absence. "I think he just got tired of the bed in the den. You know, he does have a nice apartment that he's paying rent for. I suspect he felt he needed to get back to his things."

"If you married him, then he could sleep on your new bed and move his stuff in here," Steven suggested, feigning idle interest in the conversation while he worked on a historical stage scene that he was creating in a cardboard box.

"Who mentioned anything about marriage?" Morgan asked tightly.

"Everybody," Matt answered her. "C.J. thinks it's a great idea, and so does Grams. Uncle Ross thinks you're marrying below yourself, and Gramps says everyone should mind their own business."

Three cheers for Gramps, Morgan thought dryly. She would kill her mother. The thought of her whole family sitting around discussing her love life appalled her. "Whether I get married or not is my decision, don't you think?" she asked rhetorically. As soon as the words left her mouth she knew she'd made a mistake.

"No." Steven no longer toyed with his project. He looked accusingly at her instead.

"It's a house decision," Amanda came down firmly with Steven.

"I agree. Let's take a vote," Matt said, adding his view.

"Does C.J. get a vote?" Amanda asked.

"No, he only lives here sometimes. This is just for the family," Matt decreed, laying down the rules. "I'll cast McGee's vote—I'm the oldest."

"McGee only gets a half vote," Steven argued.

"Stop. All of you stop. I will decide if I marry. This is not a voting issue." Morgan tried very hard to see something amusing in the situation. She knew it was there somewhere, but when she'd spent the afternoon painfully searching her soul, she found it hard to find any virtue in letting a dog contribute to deciding her future.

"It is not. It's our house and if you marry him he'll be our dad. It's not fair that you're the only one to decide. We want him." Matt stood with clenched fists held tightly against his sides, glaring at her from behind the table.

Not able to stand it any longer, Morgan went to the closet, grabbed her coat and car keys, and walked out of the house.

ALMOST A WEEK LATER, Morgan sat at her desk filling in student grades on the list that had to be turned in to the administration office. When she got to Trace's name she hesitated. He'd done well on the final. A low B on a comprehensive final was an impressive feat for someone who hadn't even owned the book for more than half the semester.

That B coupled with two Fs and the C he'd gotten on the infamous diet history left him with a very low D. Glancing at the computer printout, she noted that he hadn't switched to credit/no credit, either. She was going to have to give the man she loved a D.

Forcefully putting her pen to the little box after his student number she entered his grade. She was honestly surprised when she saw the A.

She stared at the unethical grade. She was a professor in a respected university. Unearned grades just weren't handed out. It wasn't fair to the other students, to her colleagues or to her profession.

There was very little that was fair about this situation, she told herself, no longer thinking about the dishonest grade. C.J. had been the first to descend on her, calling her, among other things, a chicken. After ripping into her and insulting her intelligence as well as anything else he could think of, he'd patted her head and told her to go ahead and get married—after all it couldn't be much worse than a trip to the dentist.

Her mother hadn't gone quite as far as to rue the day she was born, but she hadn't stopped much short of that, either. A number of nasty comments about all her brains and not one iota of intelligence had conveyed her mother's position clearly.

Her kids, as could have been expected, were the worst. Amanda sighed and dabbed a tissue to her eyes every time she could catch her mother's attention. She was the best of the lot. Steven had drawn up papers suing her. She wasn't clear about the grounds—breach of promise, violation of sacred trust, pain and suffering, life-long loss of a male role model—all seemed to figure prominently. Matt showed his displeasure by fighting with her over anything. Carrying out the garbage or closing the front door became major battles.

She didn't need them hounding her. She was doing a good enough job of that herself, she thought, looking at the computer card she had propped on her desk. During the final, she'd handed out the computer class evaluation cards. In a class this size almost everything was done by computer, but the students were given the opportunity to write comments on the backs of their anonymous cards with the assurance that she would read them. The card she looked at now was blank except for the words "Marry Me" written in number-two pencil.

Looking down at the grade sheet again, she chewed the end of her pen. It was just plain unethical and without any justification, but it was her class, and she'd do what she wanted. And what she wanted to do was to give the man an A. With a flourish she outlined the grade three times, making it very dark and unmistakable.

Once she'd made her grand gesture, a smile started growing slowly on her face. If she was willing to risk her position to give him a grade that he certainly hadn't earned and that he really didn't care very much about, then why was she even hesitating about risking her heart for something they both cared a whole lot about? In ten years she'd probably have some rare sun allergy and wouldn't be able to take a South Seas cruise anyway.

Rummaging through a desk drawer, she found what she was looking for. On her desk she had a stack of self-addressed postcards that a few students, who couldn't wait to learn their grades, had given her. She'd pretend that Trace was one of those red-hots and send him his grade. Addressing the blank postcard to him at the police station, she flipped it over and wrote in red ink, A. "Any concerns regarding final grade must be handled in person at Dr. Harris's office during the next two afternoons. Dr. Harris will be waiting impatiently."

Smiling happily to herself, she shrugged on her coat and left the building to hike through the snow to an off-campus mailbox. No way would she trust this particular piece of correspondence to the campus mail.

"YES, I CAN SEE that you're upset about your final grade, but it's too late to even consider submitting an extra credit project." Morgan explained patiently to the young man who sat across from her with such a hangdog look that she was sure he'd practiced it. "If you are really that unhappy with your grade, I can only suggest that you repeat the class. Both grades will show up on your transcript, but only the second will be computed into your grade point."

"But I can't fit it into my schedule next semester. I'm a graduating senior," he announced with as much grandeur as if he were introducing himself as the Prince of Wales.

"You heard the professor." Trace's voice came from the doorway. "She's not giving away any extra points," he stated emphatically. "If you'll excuse us, I have a meeting scheduled with the doctor."

Hearing, and giving way to the intimidation implicit in the older man's manner, Morgan's student quickly gathered his things and left the room.

"Did you have something you needed to discuss with me?" Morgan asked the man who had taken the chair her student had just vacated.

"Yes, Professor." A smile touched the corners of his lips. "I was wondering what it took to get an A+ in your basic nutrition class."

"I'm sorry." Morgan bit back her own smile and tried to look sincere. "In a class as large as that one, there are no opportunities to do extra credit. I'm afraid the best you can get is a straight A."

"I'm a graduating senior," he responded, mimicking the other student. "I need an A+ and I'm willing to work hard to earn it."

Morgan clicked her tongue against the roof of her mouth. "It's just not possible. No, wait. Maybe there is something." She looked at him as if deciding whether or not to make the suggestion to him. "How would you feel about taking on one slightly worn professor, three kids, assorted family members and a dog?" she questioned, her eyes shining. He looked so good that she could hardly stand this game.

"For how long?" he inquired.

"About a lifetime," she drawled seductively.

"Is this a legal thing we're talking about?" He looked as tense as a lion about ready to spring, she noted with some surprise.

"Very legal," she assured him, smiling happily.

"Okay, for the sake of my grade point, I'll do about anything," he confessed matter-of-factly, before gliding out of the chair and across to her.

At his movement, Morgan stood up and walked into his arms. Holding her tightly, as if he were afraid to let her go, he growled into her hair, "You sure took your sweet time making up your mind."

"Are you complaining?" she asked, lifting her head and kissing his neck.

"No, I love you. I'm just glad that you finally got around to admitting that you loved me, too."

"Oh, I think I've known that I loved you for a long time. Certainly by the time you arrested my son. I'm just such a coward that it took me forever to face up to my insecurities. But I'm sure now. I'm very sure." She reached up to him and caught his face between her hands, guiding him down until she could reach his lips.

After a long satisfying kiss, Trace raised his head again. "Of course, by taking so long you used up all the time you had, so now we'll have to get married next week."

"That's too soon, and it's Christmas week. I can't be ready by then," Morgan protested before his lips touched hers. Pulling away from him after an undeterminable time, she laid her head against the chest that felt so familiar and comfortable to her.

"Next week," he repeated, tightening his arms around her possessively.

"Okay," she sighed lovingly. "But you tell my mom that she can't have a big wedding this time, either," she bargained.

"Deal," he agreed, kissing the top of her head.

"Want to go try out my new bed?" Morgan suggested hopefully.

"Next week. I'm a family man with responsibilities, you know," he told her piously. "This week we use my apartment."

"Deal," Morgan responded happily, secure in the knowledge that no matter how hastily the wedding was tossed together, this marriage would be one that lasted a lifetime.

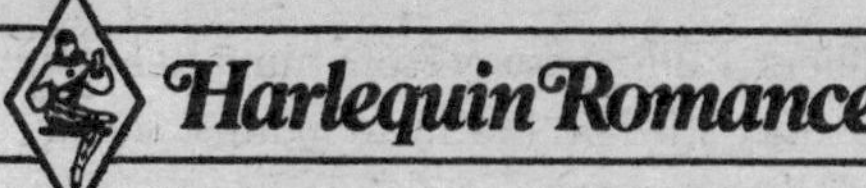

Enter the world of Romance...
Harlequin Romance

Delight in the exotic yet innocent love stories of Harlequin Romance.

Be whisked away to dazzling international capitals...or quaint European villages.

Experience the joys of falling in love...for the first time, the best time!

Six new titles every month for your reading enjoyment. Available wherever paperbacks are sold.

Rom-1

ATTRACTIVE, SPACE SAVING BOOK RACK

Display your most prized novels on this handsome and sturdy book rack. The hand-rubbed walnut finish will blend into your library decor with quiet elegance, providing a practical organizer for your favorite hard-or soft-covered books.

To order, rush your name, address and zip code, along with a check or money order for $10.70* ($9.95 plus 75¢ postage and handling) payable to *Harlequin Reader Service*:

Harlequin Reader Service
Book Rack Offer
901 Fuhrmann Blvd.
P.O. Box 1396
Buffalo, NY 14269-1396

Offer not available in Canada.

BKR-1A

*New York and Iowa residents add appropriate sales tax.

MAIL-IN-OFFER

OFFER CERTIFICATE

I have enclosed the required number of proofs of purchase from any specially marked "Gifts From The Heart" Harlequin romance book, plus cash register receipts and a check or money order payable to Harlequin Gifts From The Heart Offer, to cover postage and handling.

002

CHECK ONE	ITEM	# OF PROOFS OF PURCHASE	POSTAGE & HANDLING FEE
	01 Brass Picture Frame	2	$ 1.00
	02 Heart-Shaped Candle Holders with Candles	3	$ 1.00
	03 Heart-Shaped Keepsake Box	4	$ 1.00
	04 Gold-Plated Heart Pendant	5	$ 1.00
	05 Collectors' Doll Limited quantities available	12	$ 2.75

NAME ________________________________

STREET ADDRESS ____________________ APT. # _____

CITY ______________ STATE ________ ZIP ________

Mail this certificate, designated number of proofs of purchase (inside back page) and check or money order for postage and handling to:

Gifts From The Heart, P.O. Box 4814
Reidsville, N. Carolina 27322-4814

NOTE THIS IMPORTANT OFFER'S TERMS

Requests must be postmarked by May 31, 1988. Only proofs of purchase from specially marked "Gifts From The Heart" Harlequin books will be accepted. This certificate plus cash register receipts and a check or money order to cover postage and handling must accompany your request and may not be reproduced in any manner. Offer void where prohibited, taxed or restricted by law. LIMIT ONE REQUEST PER NAME, FAMILY, GROUP, ORGANIZATION OR ADDRESS. Please allow up to 8 weeks after receipt of order for shipment. Offer only good in the U.S.A. Hurry—Limited quantities of collectors' doll available. Collectors' dolls will be mailed to first 15,000 qualifying submitters. All other submitters will receive 12 free previously unpublished Harlequin books and a postage & handling refund.

OFFER-1RR

Take 4 best-selling love stories FREE

Plus get a FREE surprise gift!

Special Limited-Time Offer

Mail to **Harlequin Reader Service®**

In the U.S.
901 Fuhrmann Blvd.
P.O. Box 1867
Buffalo, N.Y. 14269-1867

In Canada
P.O. Box 609
Fort Erie, Ontario
L2A 5X3

YES! Please send me 4 free Harlequin American Romance® novels and my free surprise gift. Then send me 4 brand-new novels every month as they come off the presses. Bill me at the low price of $2.49 each*—a 9% saving off the retail price. There are no shipping, handling or other hidden costs. There is no minimum number of books I must purchase. I can always return a shipment and cancel at any time. Even if I never buy another book from Harlequin, the 4 free novels and the surprise gift are mine to keep forever. 154 BPA BP7F

*Plus 49¢ postage and handling per shipment in Canada.

Name (PLEASE PRINT)

Address Apt. No.

City State/Prov. Zip/Postal Code

This offer is limited to one order per household and not valid to present subscribers. Price is subject to change. AR-SUB-1C

With proofs of purchase plus postage and handling

A. **Hand-polished solid brass picture frame 1-5/8″ × 1-3/8″ with 2 proofs of purchase.**

B. **Individually handworked, pair of heart-shaped glass candle holders (2″ diameter), 6″ candles included, with 3 proofs of purchase.**

C. **Heart-shaped porcelain keepsake box (1″ high) with delicate flower motif with 4 proofs of purchase.**

D. **Radiant gold-plated heart pendant on 16″ chain with complimentary satin pouch with 5 proofs of purchase.**

E. **Beautiful collectors' doll with genuine porcelain face, hands and feet, and a charming heart appliqué on dress with 12 proofs of purchase. Limited quantities available. See offer terms.**

HERE IS HOW TO GET YOUR FREE GIFTS

Send us the required number of proofs of purchase (below) of specially marked "Gifts From The Heart" Harlequin books and cash register receipts with the Offer Certificate (available in the back pages) properly completed, plus a check or money order (do not send cash) payable to Harlequin Gifts From The Heart Offer. We'll RUSH you your specified gift. Hurry—Limited quantities of collectors' doll available. See offer terms.

ONE PROOF OF PURCHASE

To collect your free gift by mail you must include the necessary number of proofs of purchase with order certificate.